Charlie and the Great Glass Elevator

KNOPF BOOKS BY ROALD DAHL

Charlie and the Chocolate Factory

Charlie and the Great Glass Elevator

Danny the Champion of the World

The Enormous Crocodile

Fantastic Mr. Fox

George's Marvelous Medicine

James and the Giant Peach

The Mildenhall Treasure

Roald Dahl's Revolting Rhymes

The Wonderful Story of Henry Sugar and Six More

ROALD DAHL

Charlie and the Great Glass Elevator

THE FURTHER ADVENTURES OF CHARLIE BUCKET AND WILLY WONKA, CHOCOLATE-MAKER EXTRAORDINARY

Illustrated by Quentin Blake

ALFRED A. KNOPF
New York

THIS IS A BORZOI BOOK PUBLISHED BY ALFRED A. KNOPF

www.randomhouse.com/kids

Library of Congress Cataloging-in-Publication Data
Dahl, Roald.
Charlie and the great glass elevator / by Roald Dahl ; illustrated by Quentin Blake.
p. cm.
Summary: Taking up where Charlie and the Chocolate Factory leaves off, Charlie, his family, and
Mr. Wonka find themselves launched into space in the great glass elevator.
[1. Outer space—Fiction. 2. Science fiction. 3. Humorous stories.] I. Blake, Quentin, ill.
II. Title.
PZ7.D1515 Ck 2001
[Fic]—dc21   2001029347

ISBN 0-375-81525-2 (trade)
ISBN 0-375-91525-7 (lib. bdg.)

Printed in the United States of America

September 2001

10 9 8 7 6 5 4 3 2 1

Revised Edition

For my daughters
Tessa   Ophelia   Lucy

And for my godson
Edmund Pollinger

CONTENTS

1
Mr. Wonka Goes Too Far

THE LAST TIME WE SAW CHARLIE, he was riding high above his home town in the Great Glass Elevator. Only a short while before, Mr. Wonka had told him that the whole gigantic fabulous Chocolate Factory was his, and now our small friend was returning in triumph with his entire family to take over. The passengers in the Elevator (just to remind you) were:

Charlie Bucket,
  our hero.
Mr. Willy Wonka,
  chocolate-maker extraordinary.
Mr. and Mrs. Bucket,
  Charlie's father and mother.
Grandpa Joe and Grandma Josephine,
  Mr. Bucket's father and mother.
Grandpa George and Grandma Georgina,
  Mrs. Bucket's father and mother.

Grandma Josephine, Grandma Georgina and Grandpa George were still in bed, the bed having been pushed on board just before take off. Grandpa Joe, as you remember, had gotten out of bed to go around the Chocolate Factory with Charlie.

The Great Glass Elevator was a thousand feet up and cruising nicely. The sky was a brilliant blue. Everybody on board was wildly excited at the thought of going to live in the famous Chocolate Factory. Grandpa Joe was singing. Charlie was jumping up and down. Mr. and Mrs. Bucket were smiling for the first time in years, and the three old ones in the bed were grinning at one another with pink toothless gums.

"What in the world keeps this thing up in the air?" croaked Grandma Josephine.

"Skyhooks," said Mr. Wonka.

"You amaze me," said Grandma Josephine.

"Dear lady," said Mr. Wonka, "you are new to the scene. When you have been with us a little longer, nothing will amaze you."

"These skyhooks," said Grandma Josephine. "I assume

one end is hooked onto this contraption we're riding in. Right?"

"Right," said Mr. Wonka.

"What's the other end hooked onto?" said Grandma Josephine.

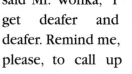

"Every day," said Mr. Wonka, "I get deafer and deafer. Remind me, please, to call up my ear doctor the moment we get back."

"Charlie," said Grandma Josephine. "I don't think I trust this gentleman very much."

"Nor do I," said Grandma Georgina. "He footles around."

Charlie leaned over the bed and whispered to the two old women. "Please," he said, "don't spoil everything. Mr. Wonka is a fantastic man. He's my friend. I love him."

"Charlie's right," whispered Grandpa Joe, joining the group. "Now you be quiet, Josie, and don't make trouble."

"We must hurry!" said Mr. Wonka. "We have so much time and so little to do! No! Wait! Strike that! Reverse it! Thank you! Now back to the factory!" he cried, clapping his hands once and springing two feet in the air with two feet. "Back we fly to the factory! But we must go *up* before we can come down! We must go *higher and higher*!"

"What did I tell you!" said Grandma Josephine. "The man's cracked!"

"Be quiet, Josie," said Grandpa Joe. "Mr. Wonka knows exactly what he's doing."

"He's cracked as a crab!" said Grandma Georgina.

"We must go higher!" said Mr. Wonka. "We must go tremendously high! Hold onto your stomachs!" He pressed a brown button. The Elevator shuddered, and then with a fearful whooshing noise it shot vertically upward like a rocket. Everybody clutched hold of everybody else and as the great machine gathered speed, the rushing whooshing sound of the wind outside grew louder and louder and shriller and shriller until it became a piercing shriek and you had to yell to make yourself heard.

"Stop!" yelled Grandma Josephine. "Joe, you make him stop! I want to get off!"

"Save us!" yelled Grandma Georgina.

"Go down!" yelled Grandpa George.

"No, no!" Mr. Wonka yelled back. "We've got to go up!"

"But why?" they all shouted at once. "Why up and not down?"

"Because the higher we are when we start coming down, the faster we'll be going when we hit," said Mr. Wonka. "We've got to be going at an absolutely sizzling speed when we hit!"

"When we hit *what?*" they cried.

"The factory, of course," answered Mr. Wonka.

"You must be whackers!" said Grandma Josephine. "We'll all be pulpified!"

"We'll be scrambled like eggs!" said Grandma Georgina.

"That," said Mr. Wonka, "is a chance we shall have to take."

"You're joking," said Grandma Josephine. "Tell us you're joking."

"Madam," said Mr. Wonka, "I never joke."

"Oh, my dears!" cried Grandma Georgina. "We'll be *lixivated*, every one of us!"

"More than likely," said Mr. Wonka.

Grandma Josephine screamed and disappeared under the bedclothes. Grandma Georgina clutched Grandpa George so tight he changed shape. Mr. and Mrs. Bucket stood hugging each other, speechless with fright. Only Charlie and Grandpa Joe kept moderately cool. They had traveled a long way with Mr. Wonka and had grown accustomed to surprises. But as the Great Elevator continued to streak upward, farther and farther away from the earth, even Charlie began to feel a trifle nervous. "Mr. Wonka!" he yelled above the noise. "What I don't understand is *why* we've got to come down at such a terrific speed."

"My dear boy," Mr. Wonka answered, "if we don't come down at a terrific speed, we'll never burst our way back in through the roof of the factory. It's not easy to punch a hole in a roof as strong as that."

"But there's a hole in it already," said Charlie. "We made it when we came out."

"Then we shall make another," said Mr. Wonka. "Two holes are better than one. Any mouse will tell you that."

Higher and higher rushed the Great Glass Elevator until soon they could see the countries and oceans of the earth spread out below them like a map. It was all very beautiful, but when you are standing on a glass floor looking down, it gives you a nasty feeling. Even Charlie was beginning to feel frightened now. He hung on tightly to Grandpa Joe's hand and looked up anxiously into the old man's face. "I'm scared, Grandpa," he said.

Grandpa Joe put an arm around Charlie's shoulders

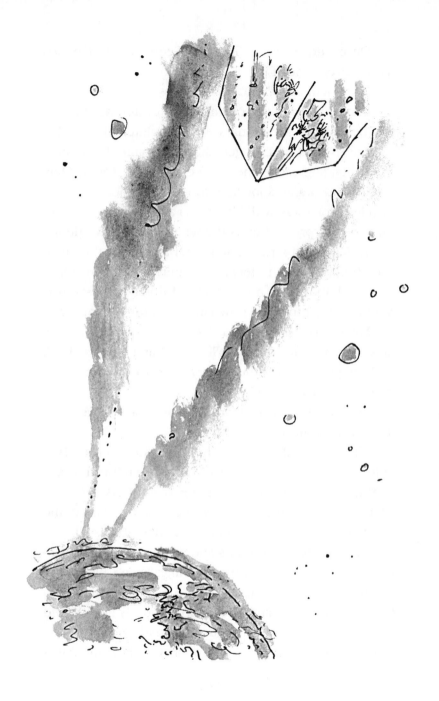

and held him close. "So am I, Charlie," he said.

"Mr. Wonka!" Charlie shouted. "Don't you think this is about high enough?"

"Very nearly," Mr. Wonka answered. "But not quite. Don't talk to me now, please. Don't disturb me. I must watch things very carefully at this stage. Split-second timing, my boy, that's what it's got to be. You see this green button. I must press it at exactly the right instant. If I'm just half a second late, then we'll go *too high!*"

"What happens if we go too high?" asked Grandpa Joe.

"Do please stop talking and let me concentrate!" Mr. Wonka said.

At that precise moment, Grandma Josephine poked her head out from under the sheets and peered over the edge of the bed. Through the glass floor she saw the entire continent of North America nearly two hundred miles below and looking no bigger than a piece of candy. "*Someone's* got to stop this maniac," she screeched, and she shot out a wrinkled old hand and grabbed Mr. Wonka by the coattails and yanked him backward onto the bed.

"No, no," cried Mr. Wonka, struggling to free himself. "Let me go! I have things to see to! Don't disturb the pilot!"

"You madman," shrieked Grandma Josephine, shaking Mr. Wonka so fast that his head became a blur. "You get us back home this instant!"

"Let me go!" cried Mr. Wonka. "I've got to press that button or we'll go too high! Let me go! Let me go!" But Grandma Josephine hung on. "Charlie!" shouted Mr. Wonka. "Press the button! The green one! Quick, quick, quick!"

Charlie leaped across the Elevator and banged his

thumb down on the green button. But as he did so, the Elevator gave a mighty groan and rolled over onto its side, and the rushing whooshing noise stopped altogether and an eerie silence took its place.

"Too late!" cried Mr. Wonka. "Oh, my goodness me, we're cooked!" As he spoke, the bed with the three old ones in it and Mr. Wonka on top lifted gently off the floor and hung suspended in mid-air. Charlie and Grandpa Joe and Mr. and Mrs. Bucket also floated upward so that in a twink the entire company, as well as the bed, were floating around like balloons inside the Great Glass Elevator.

"*Now* look what you've done!" said Mr. Wonka, floating about.

"What happened?" Grandma Josephine called out. She

had floated clear of the bed and was hovering near the ceiling in her nightshirt.

"Did we go too far?" Charlie asked.

"Too *far?*" cried Mr. Wonka. "I'll say we went too far! You know where we've gone, my friends? We've gone into orbit!"

They gaped, they gasped, they stared. They were too flabbergasted to speak.

"We are now rushing around the earth at seventeen thousand miles an hour," Mr. Wonka said. "How does that grab you?"

"I'm choking!" gasped Grandma Georgina. "I can't breathe!"

"Of course you can't," said Mr. Wonka. "There's no air up here." He sort of swam across under the ceiling to a button marked OXYGEN. He pressed it. "You'll be all right now," he said. "Breathe away."

"This is the queerest feeling," Charlie said, swimming about. "I feel like a bubble."

"It's great," said Grandpa Joe. "It feels as though I don't weigh anything at all."

"You don't," said Mr. Wonka. "None of us weighs anything—not even one ounce."

"What piffle!" said Grandma Georgina. "I weigh eighty-seven pounds exactly."

"Not now you don't," said Mr. Wonka. "You are completely weightless."

The three old ones, Grandpa George, Grandma Georgina and Grandma Josephine were trying frantically to get back into the bed, but without success. The bed was floating about in mid-air. They, of course, were also floating, and every time they got above the bed and tried to lie down, they simply floated up out of it. Charlie and Grandpa Joe were hooting with laughter. "What's so funny?" said Grandma Josephine.

"We've got you out of bed at last," said Grandpa Joe.

"Shut up and help us back!" snapped Grandma Josephine.

"Forget it," said Mr. Wonka. "You'll never stay down. Just keep floating around and be happy."

"The man's a madman!" cried Grandma Georgina. "Watch out, I say, or he'll lixivate the lot of us!"

2
Space Hotel "U.S.A."

MR. WONKA'S GREAT GLASS ELEVATOR was not the only thing orbiting the earth at that particular time. Two days earlier, the United States of America had successfully launched its first Space Hotel, a gigantic sausage-shaped capsule no less than one thousand feet long. It was called Space Hotel "U.S.A." and it was the marvel of the space age. It had inside it a tennis court, a swimming pool, a gymnasium, a children's playroom and five hundred luxury bedrooms, each with a private bath. It was fully air-conditioned. It was also equipped with a gravity-making machine so that you didn't float about inside it. You could walk normally.

This extraordinary object was now speeding round

and round the earth at a height of two hundred and forty miles. Guests were to be taken up and down by a taxi service of commuter capsules blasting off from Cape Kennedy every hour on the hour, Monday through Friday. But as yet there was nobody on board at all, not even an astronaut. The reason for this was that no one had really believed such an enormous thing would ever get off the ground without blowing up.

But the launching had been a great success and now that the Space Hotel was safely in orbit, there was a tremendous hustle and bustle to send up the first guests. It was rumored that the President of the United States himself was going to be among the first to stay in the hotel, and of course there was a mad rush by all sorts of other people across the world to book rooms. Several kings and queens had cabled the White House in Washington for reservations, and a Texas millionaire called Orson Cart, who was about to marry a Hollywood starlet called Helen Highwater, was offering one hundred thousand dollars a day for the honeymoon suite.

But you cannot send guests to a hotel unless there are lots of people there to look after them, and that explains why there was yet another interesting object orbiting the earth at that moment. This was the large Commuter Capsule containing the entire staff for Space Hotel "U.S.A." There were managers, assistant managers, desk clerks, waitresses, bellhops, chambermaids, pastry chefs and hall porters. The capsule they were traveling in was manned by the three famous astronauts, Shuckworth, Shanks and Showler, all of them handsome, clever and brave.

"In exactly one hour," said Shuckworth, speaking to the

passengers over the loudspeaker, "we shall link up with Space Hotel 'U.S.A.,' your happy home for the next ten years. And any moment now, if you look straight ahead, you should catch your first glimpse of this magnificent spaceship. Ah-ha! I see something there! That must be it, folks! There's definitely something up there ahead of us!"

Shuckworth, Shanks and Showler, as well as the managers, assistant managers, desk clerks, waitresses, bellhops, chambermaids, pastry chefs, hall porters, all stared excitedly through the windows. Shuckworth fired a couple of small rockets to make the capsule go faster, and they began to catch up very quickly.

"Hey," yelled Showler. "That isn't our Space Hotel."

"Holy rats!" cried Shanks. "What in the name of Nebuchadnezzar is it?"

"Quick! Give me the telescope!" yelled Shuckworth. With one hand, he focused the telescope and with the other he flipped the switch connecting him to Ground Control.

"Hello, Houston!" he cried into the mike. "There's something crazy going on up here. There's a thing orbiting ahead of us and it's not like any spaceship I've ever seen, that's for sure!"

"Describe it at once," ordered Ground Control in Houston.

"It's . . . it's all made of glass and it's kind of square and it's got lots of people inside it! They're all floating about like fish in a tank!"

"How many astronauts on board?"

"None," said Shuckworth. "They can't possibly be astronauts."

"What makes you say that?"

"Because at least three of them are in nightshirts!"

"Don't be a fool, Shuckworth!" snapped Ground Control. "Pull yourself together, man! This is serious!"

"I swear it!" cried poor Shuckworth. "There's three of them in nightshirts! Two old women and one old man! I can see them clearly! I can even see their faces! Jeepers, they're older than Moses! They're about ninety years old!"

"You've gone mad, Shuckworth," shouted Ground Control. "You're fired. Give me Shanks!"

"Shanks speaking," said Shanks. "Now listen here, Houston. There's these three old birds in nightshirts floating around in this crazy glass box and there's a funny little guy with a pointed beard wearing a black top hat and a plum-colored velvet tailcoat and bottle-green trousers . . ."

"Stop!" screamed Ground Control.

"Hold the phone!" said Shanks. "There's also a little boy about ten years old."

"That's no boy, you idiot!" shouted Ground Control. "That's an astronaut in disguise! It's a midget astronaut dressed up as a little boy! Those old people are astronauts too! They're all in disguise!"

"But who *are* they?" cried Shanks.

"How the heck would I know?" said Ground Control. "Are they heading for our Space Hotel?"

"That's exactly where they are heading," cried Shanks. "I can see the Space Hotel now about a mile ahead."

"They're going to blow it up!" yelled Ground Control. "This is desperate! This is . . ." Suddenly his voice was cut off and Shanks heard another quite different voice in his earphones. It was deep and rasping.

"I'll take charge of this," said the deep rasping voice. "Are you there, Shanks?"

"Of course I'm here," said Shanks. "But how dare you butt in! Keep your big nose out of this! Who are you anyway?"

"This is the President of the United States," said the voice.

"And this is the Wizard of Oz," said Shanks. "Who are you kidding?"

"Cut the piffle, Shanks!" snapped the President. "This is a national emergency!"

"Good grief!" said Shanks, turning to Shuckworth and Showler. "It really *is* the President. It's President Gilligrass himself! Well, *hello there*, Mr. President, sir. How are *you* today?"

"How many people are there in that glass capsule?" rasped the President.

"Eight," said Shanks. "All floating."

"Floating?!"

"We're outside the pull of gravity up here, Mr. President. Everything floats. We'd be floating ourselves if we weren't strapped down. Didn't you know that?"

"Of course I knew it," said the President. "What else can you tell me about that glass capsule?"

"There's a bed in it," said Shanks. "A big double bed, and that's floating too."

"A bed?" barked the President. "Whoever heard of a bed in a spacecraft!"

"I swear it's a bed!" said Shanks.

"You must be loopy, Shanks!" declared the President. "You're dotty as a doughnut! Let me talk to Showler!"

"Showler here, Mr. President," said Showler, taking the mike from Shanks. "It is a great honor to talk to you, Mr. President, sir."

"Oh, shut up!" said the President. "Just tell me what you see."

"It's a bed all right, Mr. President. I can see it through my telescope. It's got sheets and blankets and a mattress . . ."

"That's not a bed, you driveling thickwit!" yelled the President. "Can't you understand it's a trick! It's a bomb! It's a bomb disguised as a bed! They're going to blow up our magnificent Space Hotel!"

"Who's *they*, Mr. President, sir?" said Showler.

"Don't talk so much and let me think!" said the President. There were a few moments of silence. Showler waited tensely. So did Shanks and Shuckworth. So did the managers and assistant managers and desk clerks and waitresses and bellhops and chambermaids and pastry chefs and hall porters. And down in the huge Control Room at Houston, one hundred controllers sat motionless in front of their dials and monitors, waiting to see what orders the President would give next to the astronauts.

"I've just thought of something," said the President. "Don't you have a television camera up there on the front of your spacecraft, Showler?"

"Sure do, Mr. President."

"Then switch it on, you nit, and let all of us down here get a look at this object!"

"I never thought of that," said Showler. "No *wonder* you're the President. Here goes!" He reached out and switched on the T.V. camera in the nose of the spacecraft, and at that moment, five hundred million people all over the world who had been listening in on their radios, rushed to their television sets.

On their screens they saw exactly what Shuckworth and Shanks and Showler were seeing—a weird glass box in splendid orbit around the earth, and inside the box, seen not too clearly but seen nonetheless, were seven grown-ups and one small boy and a big double bed, all floating. Three of the grown-ups were barelegged and wearing nightshirts. And far off in the distance, beyond the glass box, the T.V. watchers could see the enormous, glistening, silvery shape of Space Hotel "U.S.A."

But it was the sinister glass box itself that everyone was staring at, and the cargo of sinister creatures inside it—eight astronauts so tough and strong they didn't even bother to wear spacesuits. Who were these people and where did they come from? And what in heaven's name was that big evil-looking thing disguised as a double bed? The President had said it was a bomb and he was probably right. But what were they going to do with it? All across America and Canada and Russia and Japan and India and China and Africa and England and France and Germany and everywhere else in the world a kind of panic began to take hold of the television watchers.

"Keep well clear of them, Showler!" ordered the President over the radio link.

"Sure will, Mr. President!" Showler answered. "I *sure will*!"

3
The Link-Up

INSIDE THE GREAT GLASS ELEVATOR there was also a good deal of excitement. Charlie and Mr. Wonka and all the others could see clearly the huge silvery shape of Space Hotel "U.S.A." about a mile ahead of them. And behind them was the smaller (but still pretty enormous) Commuter Capsule. The Great Glass Elevator (not looking at all great now beside these two monsters) was in the middle. And of course everybody, even Grandma Josephine, knew very well what was going on. They even knew that the three astronauts in charge of the Commuter Capsule were called Shuckworth, Shanks and Showler. The whole world knew about these things. Newspapers and television had been shouting about almost nothing else for the past six months. Operation Space Hotel was the event of the century.

"What a load of luck!" cried Mr. Wonka. "We've landed

ourselves slap in the middle of the biggest space operation of all time!"

"We've landed ourselves in the middle of a nasty
mess!" said Grandma Josephine. "Turn back at once!"

"*No,* Grandma," said Charlie. "We've *got* to watch it
now! We *must* see the Commuter Capsule linking up
with the Space Hotel!"

Mr. Wonka floated right up close to Charlie. "Let's beat
them to it, Charlie," he whispered. "Let's get there first
and go aboard the Space Hotel ourselves!"

Charlie gaped. Then he gulped. Then he said softly,
"It's impossible. You've got to have all sorts of special gad-
gets to link up with another spacecraft, Mr. Wonka."

"My Elevator could link up with a crocodile if it had
to," said Mr. Wonka. "Just leave it to me, my boy!"

"Grandpa Joe!" cried Charlie. "Did you hear that? We're
going to link up with the Space Hotel and go on board!"

"Yippeeeeee!" shouted Grandpa Joe. "What a brilliant
thought, sir! What a staggering idea!" He grabbed Mr.
Wonka's hand and started shaking it like a thermometer.

"Be quiet, you balmy old bat!" said Grandma Josephine.
"We're in a hot enough stew already! I want to go home!"

"Me, too!" said Grandma Georgina.

"What if they come after us?" said Mr. Bucket, speaking
for the first time.

"What if they capture us?" said Mrs. Bucket.

"What if they shoot us?" said Grandma Georgina.

"What if my beard were made of green spinach?" cried
Mr. Wonka. "Bunkum and tummyrot! You'll never get anywhere if you go about what-iffing like that. Would Colum-
bus have discovered America if he'd said 'What if I sink on

the way over? What if I meet pirates? What if I never come back?' He wouldn't even have started! We want no what-iffers around here, right Charlie? Off we go, then! But wait . . . this is a very tricky maneuver and I'm going to need help. We have to press lots of buttons, all in different parts of the Elevator. I shall take those two over there, the white and the black." Mr. Wonka made a funny blowing noise with his mouth and glided effortlessly, like a huge bird, across the Elevator to the white and black buttons, and there he hovered. "Grandpa Joe, sir, kindly station yourself beside that silver button there . . . yes, that's the one. And you, Charlie, go up and stay floating beside that little golden button near the ceiling. I must tell you that each of these buttons fires booster rockets from different places outside the Elevator. That's how we change direction. Grandpa Joe's rockets turn us to starboard, to the right. Charlie's turn us to port, to the left. Mine make us go higher or lower or faster or slower. All ready?"

"No! Wait!" cried Charlie, who was floating exactly

midway between the floor and the ceiling. "How do I get up? I can't get up to the ceiling!" He was thrashing his arms and legs violently, like a drowning swimmer, but getting nowhere.

"My dear boy," said Mr. Wonka. "You can't *swim* in this stuff. It isn't water you know. It's air and very thin air at that. There's nothing to push against. So you have to use jet propulsion. Watch me. First, you take a deep breath, then you make a small round hole with your mouth and you blow as hard as you can. If you blow downward, you jet propel yourself up. If you blow left, you shoot off to the right, and so on. You maneuver yourself like a spacecraft, but using your mouth as a booster rocket."

Suddenly everyone began practicing this business of flying about, and the whole Elevator was filled with the blowings and snortings of the passengers. Grandma Georgina, in her red flannel nightgown with two skinny bare legs sticking out of the bottom was trumpeting and spitting like a rhinoceros and flying from one side of the Elevator to the other, shouting, "Out of my way! Out of my way!" and crashing into poor Mr. and Mrs. Bucket with terrible speed. Grandpa George and Grandma Josephine were doing the same. And well may you wonder what the millions of people down on earth were thinking as they watched these crazy happenings on their television screens. You must realize they couldn't see things very clearly. The Great Glass Elevator was only about the size of a grapefruit on their screens, and the people inside, slightly blurred through the glass, were no bigger than the pits of the grapefruit. Even so, the watchers below could see them buzzing about wildly like insects in a glass box.

"What in the world are they doing?" shouted the President of the United States, staring at the screen.

"Looks like some kind of a war dance, Mr. President," answered astronaut Showler over the radio.

"You mean they're Indians!" said the President.

"I didn't say that, sir."

"Oh, yes you did, Showler."

"Oh, no I didn't, Mr. President."

"Silence!" said the President. "You're muddling me up."

Back in the Elevator, Mr. Wonka was saying, "*Please! Please!* Do stop flying about! Keep still everybody, so we can get on with the docking!"

"You miserable old mackerel!" said Grandma Georgina, sailing past him. "Just when we start having a bit of fun, you want to stop it!"

"Look at me, everybody!" shouted Grandma Josephine. "I'm flying! I'm a golden eagle!"

"I can fly faster than any of you!" cried Grandpa George, whizzing round and round, his nightgown billowing out behind him like the tail of a parrot.

"Grandpa George!" cried Charlie. "Please calm down. If we don't hurry, those astronauts will get there before us. Don't you want to see inside the Space Hotel, any of you?"

"Out of my way!" shouted Grandma Georgina, blowing herself back and forth. "I'm a jumbo jet!"

"You're a balmy old bat!" said Mr. Wonka.

In the end, the old people grew tired and out of breath, and everyone settled quietly into a floating position. "All set, Charlie and Grandpa Joe, sir?" said Mr. Wonka.

"All set, Mr. Wonka," Charlie answered, hovering near the ceiling.

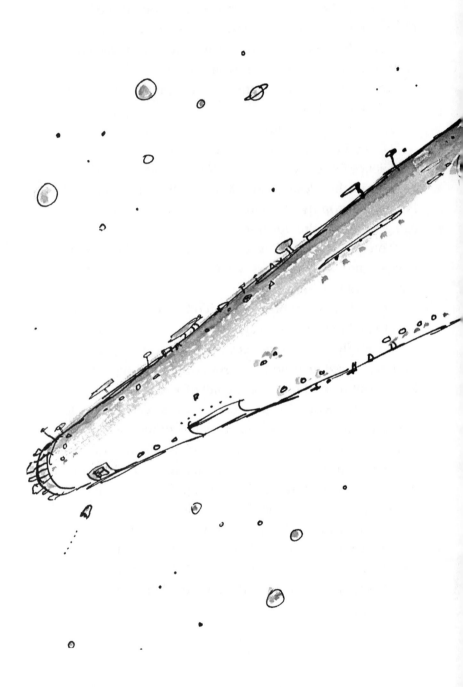

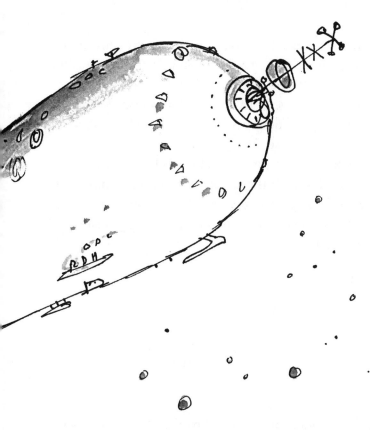

"I'll give the orders," said Mr. Wonka. "I'm the pilot. Don't fire your rockets until I tell you. And don't forget who is who. Charlie, you're port. Grandpa Joe, you're starboard." Mr. Wonka pressed one of his own two buttons and immediately booster rockets began firing underneath the Great Glass Elevator. The Elevator leaped forward, but swerved violently to the right. "Hard a-port!" yelled Mr. Wonka. Charlie pressed his button. His rockets fired. The Elevator swung back into line. "Steady as you go!" cried Mr. Wonka. "Starboard ten degrees! . . . Steady! . . . Steady! . . . Keep her there! . . ."

Soon they were hovering directly underneath the tail of the enormous silvery Space Hotel. "You see that little square door with the bolts on it?" said Mr. Wonka. "That's the docking entrance. It won't be long now. Port a fraction . . . Steady! . . . Starboard a bit! . . . Good . . . Good . . . Easy does it . . . We're nearly there . . ."

To Charlie, it felt rather as though he were in a tiny rowboat underneath the stern of the biggest ship in the world. The Space Hotel towered over them. It was enormous. "I can't wait," thought Charlie, "to get inside and see what it's like."

4
The President

HALF A MILE BACK, Shuckworth, Shanks and Showler were keeping the television camera aimed all the time at the Glass Elevator. And across the world, millions and millions of people were clustered around their T.V. screens, watching tensely the drama being acted out two hundred and forty miles above the earth. In his study in the White House sat Lancelot R. Gilligrass, President of the United States of America, the most powerful man on earth. In this moment of crisis, all his most important advisers had been summoned urgently to his presence, and there they all were now, following closely on the giant television screen every move made by this dangerous-looking glass capsule and its eight desperate-looking astronauts. The entire Cabinet was present. The Chief of the Army was there, together with four other generals. There was the Chief of the Navy and the Chief of the Air Force and a sword swallower from Afghanistan, who was the President's best friend. There was the President's Chief Financial Advisor, who was standing in the middle of the room trying to balance the budget on top of his head, but it kept falling off. Standing nearest of all to the President was the Vice-President, a huge lady of eighty-nine with a whiskery chin. She had been the President's nurse when he was a baby and her name was Miss Tibbs. Miss Tibbs was the power behind the throne. She stood no nonsense from anyone. Some people said she was as strict with the President now as when he was a little boy. She was the terror of the White House and even the Head of the F.B.I. broke into a sweat when summoned to her presence. Only the President was allowed to call her Nanny. The President's famous cat, Mrs. Taubsypuss, was also in the room.

There was absolute silence now in the Presidential study. All eyes were riveted on the T.V. screen as the small glass object, with its booster rockets firing, slid smoothly up behind the giant Space Hotel.

"They're going to link up!" shouted the President. "They're going on board our Space Hotel!"

"They're going to blow it up!" cried the Chief of the Army. "Let's blow *them* up first, crash bang wallop bang-bang-bang-bang-bang." The Chief of the Army was wearing so many medal ribbons they covered the entire front of his tunic on both sides and spread down onto his pants as well. "Come on, Mr. P.," he said. "Let's have some really super-duper explosions!"

"Silence, you silly boy!" said Miss Tibbs, and the Chief of the Army slunk into a corner.

"Listen," said the President. "The point is this. *Who are they? And where do they come from?* Where's my Chief Spy?"

"Here, sir, Mr. President, sir," said the Chief Spy. He had

a false moustache, a false beard, false eyelashes, false teeth and a falsetto voice.

"Knock-knock," said the President.

"Who's there?" said the Chief Spy.

"Courteney."

"Courteney who?"

"Courteney one yet?" said the President.

There was a brief silence.

"The President asked you a question," said Miss Tibbs in an icy voice. "Have you Courteney one yet?"

"No, ma'am, not yet," said the Chief Spy, beginning to twitch.

"Well, here's your chance," snarled Miss Tibbs.

"Quite right," said the President. "Tell me immediately who those people are in that glass capsule!"

"Ah-ha," said the Chief Spy, twirling his false moustache. "That is a very difficult question."

"You mean you don't know?"

"I mean I do know, Mr. President. At least I think I know. Listen. We have just launched the finest hotel in the world. Right?"

"Right."

"And who is so madly jealous of this wonderful hotel of ours that he wants to blow it up?"

"Miss Tibbs," said the President.

"Wrong," said the Chief Spy. "Try again."

"Well," said the President, thinking deeply. "In that case, could it not perhaps be some other hotel owner who is envious of our lovely hotel?"

"Brilliant!" cried the Chief Spy. "Go on, sir! You're getting warm!"

"It's Mr. Waldorf," said the President. "Or Mr. Astoria?"

"Warmer and warmer, Mr. President!"

"Mr. Ritz!"

"You're hot, sir! You're boiling hot! Go on!"

"I've got it!" cried the President. "It's Mr. Hilton!"

"Well done, sir!" said the Chief Spy.

"Are you sure it's him?"

"Not sure, but it's certainly a warm possibility, Mr. President. After all, Mr. Hilton's got hotels in just about every country in the world but he hasn't got one in space. And we have. He must be madder than a maggot!"

"By gum, we'll soon fix this!" snapped the President, grabbing one of the eleven telephones on his desk. "Hello," he said into the phone. "Hello hello hello! Where's the operator?" He jiggled furiously on the little thing you jiggle when you want the operator. "Operator, where are you?"

"They won't answer you now," said Miss Tibbs. "They're all watching television."

"Well, *this* one'll answer!" said the President, snatching up a bright red telephone. This was the hot line direct to the Premier of Soviet Russia in Moscow. It was always open and only used in terrible emergencies. "It's just as likely to be the Russians as Mr. Hilton," the President went on. "Don't you agree, Nanny?"

"It's bound to be the Russians," said Miss Tibbs.

"Premier Yugetoff speaking," said the voice from Moscow. "What's on your mind, Mr. President?"

"Knock-knock," said the President.

"Who's there?" said the Soviet Premier.

"Warren."

"Warren who?"

"Warren Peace by Leo Tolstoy," said the President. "Now see here, Yugetoff. You get those astronauts of yours off that Space Hotel of ours this instant! Otherwise, I'm afraid we're going to have to show you just where you get off, Yugetoff!"

"Those astronauts are not Russians, Mr. President."

"He's lying," said Miss Tibbs.

"You're lying," said the President.

"Not lying, sir," said Premier Yugetoff. "Have you looked closely at those astronauts in the glass box? I myself cannot see them too clearly on my T.V. screen, but one of them, the little one with the pointed beard and the top hat, has a distinctly Chinese look about him. In fact, he reminds me very much of my friend the Prime Minister of China."

"Great garbage!" cried the President, slamming down the red phone and picking up a porcelain one. The porcelain phone went directly to the Head of the Chinese Republic in Peking.

"Hello hello hello!" said the President.

"Wing's Fish and Vegetable Store in Shanghai," said a small distant voice. "Mr. Wing speaking."

"Nanny!" cried the President, banging down the phone. "I thought this was a direct line to the Premier!"

"It is," said Miss Tibbs. "Try again."

The President picked up the receiver. "Hello!" he yelled.

"Mr. Wong speaking," said a voice at the other end.

"Mister who?" screamed the President.

"Mr. Wong, assistant stationmaster, Chunking, and if you asking about ten o'clock tlain, ten o'clock tlain no lunning today. Boiler burst."

The President threw the phone across the room at the Postmaster General. It hit him in the stomach. "What's the matter with this thing?" shouted the President.

"It is very difficult to phone people in China, Mr. President," said the Postmaster General. "The country's so full of Wings and Wongs, every time you wing you get the wong number."

"You're not kidding," said the President.

The Postmaster General replaced the telephone on the desk. "Try it just once more, Mr. President, please," he said. "I've tightened the screws underneath."

The President again picked up the receiver.

"Gleetings, honorable Mr. Plesident," said a soft faraway voice. "Here is Assistant-Plemier Chu-On-Dat speaking. How can I do for you?"

"Knock-knock," said the President.

"Who der?"

"Ginger."

"Ginger who?"

"Ginger yourself much when you fell off the Great Wall of China?" said the President. "Okay, Chu-On-Dat. Let me speak to Premier How-Yu-Bin."

"Much regret Premier How-Yu-Bin not here just this second, Mr. Plesident."

"Where is he?"

"He outside mending a flat tire on his bicycle."

"Oh no, he isn't," said the President. "You can't fool me, you crafty old mandarin! At this very minute he's boarding our magnificent Space Hotel with seven other rascals to blow it up!"

"Excuse pleese, Mr. Plesident. You make big mistake."

"No mistake!" barked the President. "And if you don't call them off right away I'm going to tell my Chief of the Army to blow them all sky high! So chew on that, Chu-On-Dat!"

"Hooray!" said the Chief of the Army. "Let's blow everyone up! Bang-bang! Bang-bang!"

"Silence!" barked Miss Tibbs.

"I've done it!" cried the Chief Financial Adviser. "Look at me, everybody! I've balanced the budget!" And indeed he had. He stood proudly in the middle of the room with the enormous two-hundred-billion-dollar budget balanced beautifully on the top of his bald head. Everyone clapped. Then suddenly the voice of astronaut Shuckworth cut in urgently on the radio loudspeaker in the President's study. "They've linked up and gone on board!" shouted Shuckworth. "And they've taken in the bed . . . I mean the bomb!"

The President sucked in his breath sharply. He also sucked in a big fly that happened to be passing at the time. He choked. Miss Tibbs thumped him on the back. He swallowed the fly and felt better. But he was very angry. He seized pencil and paper and began to draw a picture. As he drew, he kept muttering, "I won't have flies in my office! I won't put up with them!" His advisers waited eagerly for what was coming. They knew that the great man was about to give the world yet another of his brilliant inventions. The last had been the Gilligrass Left-Handed Corkscrew, which had been hailed by left-handers across the nation as one of the greatest blessings of the century.

"There you are!" said the President, holding up the paper. "This is the Gilligrass Patent Fly-Trap!" They all crowded round to look.

"The fly climbs up the ladder on the left," said the President. "He walks along the plank. He stops. He sniffs. He smells something good. He peers over the edge and sees the sugar lump. 'Ah-ha!' he cries. 'Sugar!' He is just about to climb down the string to reach it when he sees the basin of water below. 'Ho-ho!' he says. 'It's a trap! They want me to fall in!' So he walks on, thinking what a clever fly he is. But as you see, I have left out one of the rungs in the ladder he goes down by, so he falls and breaks his neck."

"Tremendous, Mr. President!" they all exclaimed. "Fantastic! A stroke of genius!"

"I wish to order one hundred thousand for the Army immediately," said the Chief of the Army.

"Thank you," said the President, making a careful note of the order.

"I repeat," said the frantic voice of Shuckworth over the loudspeaker, "they've gone on board and taken the bomb with them!"

"Stay well clear of them, Shuckworth," ordered the

President. "There's no point in getting your boys blown up as well."

And now, all over the world, the millions of watchers waited more tensely than ever in front of their television sets. The picture on their screens, in vivid color, showed the sinister little glass box securely linked up to the underbelly of the gigantic Space Hotel. It looked like some tiny baby animal clinging to its mother. And when the camera zoomed closer, it was clear for all to see that the glass box was completely empty. All eight of the desperadoes had climbed into the Space Hotel and they had taken their bomb with them.

5

Men from Mars

THERE WAS NO FLOATING inside the Space Hotel. The gravity-making machine saw to that. So once the docking had been triumphantly achieved, Mr. Wonka, Charlie, Grandpa Joe and Mr. and Mrs. Bucket were able to walk out of the Great Glass Elevator into the lobby of the Hotel. As for Grandpa George, Grandma Georgina and Grandma Josephine, none of them had had their feet on the ground for over twenty years and they certainly weren't going to change their habits now. So when the floating stopped, they all three plopped right back into bed again and insisted that the bed, with them in it, be pushed into the Space Hotel.

Charlie gazed around the huge lobby. On the floor there was a thick green carpet. Twenty tremendous chandeliers hung shimmering from the ceiling. The walls were covered with valuable pictures and there were big soft armchairs all over the place. At the far end of the room there were five elevator doors. The group stared in silence at all this luxury. Nobody dared to speak. Mr. Wonka had warned them that every word they uttered would be picked up by Space Control in Houston, so they had better be careful. A faint humming noise came from somewhere below the floor, but that only made the silence more spooky. Charlie took hold of Grandpa Joe's hand and held it tight. He wasn't sure he liked this very much. They had broken into the greatest machine ever built by man, the property of the United States Government, and if they were discovered and captured as they surely would be in the end, what would happen to them then? Jail for life? Yes, or something worse.

Mr. Wonka was writing on a little pad. He held up the pad. It said: ANYBODY HUNGRY?

The three old ones in the bed began waving their arms and nodding and opening and shutting their mouths. Mr. Wonka turned the paper over. On the other side it said: THE KITCHENS OF THIS HOTEL ARE LOADED WITH LUSCIOUS FOOD, LOBSTERS, STEAKS, ICE CREAM. WE SHALL HAVE A FEAST TO END ALL FEASTS.

Suddenly, a tremendous booming voice came out of a loudspeaker hidden somewhere in the room. "ATTENTION!" boomed the voice, and Charlie jumped. So did Grandpa Joe. Everybody jumped, even Mr. Wonka. "ATTENTION THE EIGHT FOREIGN ASTRONAUTS! THIS IS SPACE CONTROL

IN HOUSTON, TEXAS, U.S.A.! YOU ARE TRESPASSING ON AMERICAN PROPERTY! YOU ARE ORDERED TO IDENTIFY YOURSELVES IMMEDIATELY! SPEAK NOW!"

"Ssshhh!" whispered Mr. Wonka, finger to lips.

There followed a few seconds of awful silence. Nobody moved except Mr. Wonka who kept saying "Ssshhh! Ssshhh!"

"WHO . . . ARE . . . YOU?" boomed the voice from Houston, and the whole world heard it. "I REPEAT . . . WHO . . . ARE . . . YOU?" shouted the urgent angry voice, and five hundred million people crouched in front of their television sets waiting for an answer to come from the mysterious strangers inside the Space Hotel. The television was not able to show a picture of these mysterious strangers. There was no camera in there to record the scene. Only the words came through. The T.V. watchers saw nothing but the outside of the giant hotel in orbit, photographed of course by Shuckworth, Shanks and Showler, who were following behind. For half a minute the world waited for a reply.

But no reply came.

"SPEAK!" boomed the voice, getting louder and louder and ending in a fearful frightening shout that rattled Charlie's eardrums. "SPEAK! SPEAK! SPEAK!" Grandma Georgina shot under the sheet. Grandma Josephine stuck her fingers in her ears. Grandpa George buried his head in the pillow. Mr. and Mrs. Bucket, both petrified, were once again in each other's arms. Charlie was clutching Grandpa Joe's hand, and the two of them were staring at Mr. Wonka and begging him with their eyes to do something. Mr.

Wonka stood very still, and although his face looked calm, you can be quite sure his clever inventive brain was spinning like a dynamo.

"THIS IS YOUR LAST CHANCE!" boomed the voice. "WE ARE ASKING YOU ONCE MORE . . . WHO . . . ARE . . . YOU? REPLY IMMEDIATELY! IF YOU DO NOT REPLY WE SHALL BE FORCED TO REGARD YOU AS DANGEROUS ENEMIES. WE SHALL THEN PRESS THE EMERGENCY FREEZER SWITCH AND THE TEMPERATURE IN THE SPACE HOTEL WILL DROP TO MINUS ONE HUNDRED DEGREES CENTIGRADE. ALL OF YOU WILL BE INSTANTLY DEEP-FROZEN. YOU HAVE FIFTEEN SECONDS TO SPEAK. AFTER THAT YOU WILL TURN INTO ICICLES . . . ONE . . . TWO . . . THREE . . ."

"Grandpa," whispered Charlie as the counting continued, "we must do something. We *must!* Quick!"

"SIX!" said the voice. "SEVEN! . . . EIGHT! . . . NINE! . . ."

Mr. Wonka had not moved. He was still gazing straight ahead, still quite cool, perfectly expressionless. Charlie and Grandpa Joe were staring at him in horror. Then, all at once, they saw the tiny twinkling wrinkles of a smile appear around the corners of his eyes. He sprang to life. He spun round on his toes, skipped a few paces across the floor and then, in a frenzied unearthly sort of scream, he cried, "FIMBO FEEZI!"

The loudspeaker stopped counting. There was silence. All over the world there was silence.

Charlie's eyes were riveted on Mr. Wonka. He was going to speak again. He was taking a deep breath. "BUNGO BUNI!" he screamed. He put so much force into his voice that the effort lifted him right up onto the tips of his toes.

"BUNGO BUNI
DAFU DUNI
YUBEE LUNI!"

Again the silence.

The next time Mr. Wonka spoke, the words came out

so fast and sharp and loud they were like bullets from a machine gun. "ZOONK-ZOONK-ZOONK-ZOONK-ZOONK!" he barked. The noise echoed around and around the lobby of the Space Hotel. It echoed around the world.

Mr. Wonka now turned and faced the far end of the lobby where the loudspeaker voice had come from. He walked a few paces forward as a man would, perhaps, who wanted a more intimate conversation with his audience. And this time, the tone was much quieter, the words came more slowly, but there was a touch of steel in every syllable:

"KIRASUKU MALIBUKU,
WEEBEE WIZE UN YUBEE KUKU!

ALIPENDA KAKAMENDA,
PANTZ FORLDUN IFNO SUSPENDA!

FUNIKIKA KANDERIKA,
WEEBEE STRONGA YUBEE WEEKA!

POPOKOTA BORUMOKA
VERI RISKI YU PROVOKA!

KATIKATI MOONS UN STARS
FANFANISHA VENUS MARS!"

Mr. Wonka paused dramatically for a few seconds. Then he took an enormous deep breath and in a wild and fearsome voice, he yelled out:

"KITIMBIBI ZOONK!
FIMBOLEEZI ZOONK!
GUGUMIZA ZOONK!
FUMIKAKA ZOONK!
ANAPOLALA ZOONK ZOONK ZOONK!"

The effect of all this on the world below was electric. In the Control Room in Houston, in the White House in Washington, in palaces and city buildings and mountain shacks from America to China to Peru, the five hundred million people who heard that wild and fearsome voice yelling out these strange and mystic words all shivered with fear before their television sets. Everybody began turning to everybody else and saying, "Who are they? What language was that? Where do they come from?"

In the President's study in the White House, Vice-President Tibbs, the members of the Cabinet, the Chiefs of the Army and the Navy and the Air Force, the sword swallower from Afghanistan, the Chief Financial Adviser and Mrs. Taubsypuss the cat all stood tense and rigid. They were more than a little afraid. But the President himself kept a cool head and a clear brain. "Nanny!" he cried. "Oh, Nanny, what on earth do we do now?"

"I'll get you a nice warm glass of milk," said Miss Tibbs.

"I hate the stuff," said the President. "Please don't make me drink it!"

"Then summon the Chief Interpreter," said Miss Tibbs.

"Summon the Chief Interpreter!" said the President. "Where is he?"

"Right here, Mr. President," said the Chief Interpreter.

"What language was that creature spouting up there in the Space Hotel? Be quick! Was it Eskimo?"

"Not Eskimo, Mr. President."

"Ha! Then it was Tagalog! Either Tagalog or Ugro!"

"Not Tagalog, Mr. President. Not Ugro, either."

"Was it Tulu, then? Or Tungus or Tupi?"

"Definitely not Tulu, Mr. President. And I'm quite sure it wasn't Tungus or Tupi."

"Don't stand there telling him what it *wasn't,* you idiot!" said Miss Tibbs. "Tell him what it *was!*"

"Yes, ma'am, Miss Vice-President, ma'am," said the Chief Interpreter, beginning to shake. "Believe me, Mr. President," he went on, "it was not a language I have ever heard before."

"But I thought you knew every language in the world."

"I do, Mr. President."

"Don't lie to me, Chief Interpreter. How can you possibly know every language in the world when you don't know this one?"

"It is not a language of this world, Mr. President."

"Nonsense, man!" barked Miss Tibbs. "I understood some of it myself!"

"These people, Miss Vice-President, ma'am, have obviously tried to learn just a few of our easier words, but the rest of it is a language that has never been heard before on this earth!"

"Screaming scorpions!" cried the President. "You mean to tell me they could be coming from . . . from . . . from *somewhere else?*"

"Precisely, Mr. President."

"Like where?" said the President.

"Who knows?" said the Chief Interpreter. "But did you not notice, Mr. President, how they used the words Venus and Mars?"

"Of course I noticed it," said the President. "But what's that got to do with it? . . . Ah-ha! I see what you're driving at! Good gracious me! Men from Mars!"

"And Venus," said the Chief Interpreter.

"That," said the President, "could make for trouble."

"I'll say it could!" said the Chief Interpreter.

"He wasn't talking to you," said Miss Tibbs.

"What do we do now, General?" said the President.

"Blow 'em up!" cried the General.

"You're always wanting to blow things up," said the President crossly. "Can't you think of something *else?*"

"I like blowing things up," said the General. "It makes such a lovely noise. *Woomph-woomph!*"

"Don't be a fool!" said Miss Tibbs. "If you blow these people up, Mars will declare war on us! So will Venus!"

"Quite right, Nanny," said the President. "We'd be troculated like turkeys, every one of us! We'd be mashed like potatoes!"

"I'll take 'em on!" shouted the Chief of the Army.

"Shut up!" snapped Miss Tibbs. "You're fired!"

"Hooray!" said all the other generals. "Well done, Miss Vice-President, ma'am!"

Miss Tibbs said, "We've *got* to treat these fellows gently. The one who spoke just now sounded extremely cross. We've got to be polite to them, butter them up, make them happy. The last thing we want is to be invaded by men from Mars. You've got to talk to them, Mr. President. Tell Houston we want another direct radio link with the Space Hotel! And hurry!"

6
Invitation to the White House

"THE PRESIDENT OF THE UNITED STATES will now address you!" announced the loudspeaker voice in the lobby of the Space Hotel.

Grandma Georgina's head peeped cautiously out from under the sheets. Grandma Josephine took her fingers out of her ears and Grandpa George lifted his face from the pillow.

"You mean he's actually going to speak to us?" whispered Charlie.

"Ssshhh," said Mr. Wonka. "Listen."

"Dear friends," said the well-known Presidential voice over the loudspeaker. "Dear, *dear* friends! Welcome to Space Hotel 'U.S.A.' Greetings to the brave astronauts from Mars and Venus . . ."

"Mars and Venus!" whispered Charlie. "You mean he thinks we're from . . ."

"Ssshh-ssshh-ssshh!" said Mr. Wonka. He was doubled up with silent laughter, shaking all over and hopping from one foot to the other.

"You have come a long way," the President continued, "so why don't you come just a tiny bit farther and pay *us* a visit down here on our humble little earth? I invite all eight of you to stay with me here in Washington as my honored guests. You could land that wonderful glass space machine of yours on the lawn in back of the White House. We shall have the red carpet out and ready. I do hope you know enough of our language to understand me. I shall wait most anxiously for your reply."

There was a click and the President went off the air.

"What a fantastic thing!" whispered Grandpa Joe. The White House, Charlie! We're invited to the White House as honored guests!"

Charlie caught hold of Grandpa Joe's hands and the two of them started dancing round and round the lobby of the hotel. Mr. Wonka, still shaking with laughter, went and sat down on the bed and signaled everyone to gather

round close so they could whisper without being heard by the hidden microphones.

"They're scared to death," he whispered. "They won't bother us any more now. So let's have that feast we were talking about and afterward we can explore the hotel."

"Aren't we going to the White House?" whispered Grandma Josephine. "I want to go to the White House and stay with the President."

"My dear old dotty dumpling," said Mr. Wonka. "You look as much like a man from Mars as a bedbug! They'd know at once they'd been fooled. We'd be arrested before we could say how d'you do."

Mr. Wonka was right. There could be no question of accepting the President's invitation and they all knew it.

"But we've got to say *something* to him," Charlie whispered. "He must be sitting down there in the White House this very minute waiting for an answer."

"Make an excuse," said Mr. Bucket.

"Tell him we're otherwise engaged," said Mrs. Bucket.

"Ask him for a rain check," said Grandpa Joe.

"You are right," whispered Mr. Wonka. "It is rude to ignore an invitation." He stood up and walked a few paces from the group. For a moment or two he remained quite still, gathering his thoughts. Then once again Charlie saw those tiny twinkling, smiling wrinkles around the corners of the eyes, and when he began to speak, his voice this time was like the voice of a giant, deep and devilish, very loud and very slow:

"In the quelchy quaggy sogmire,
In the mashy mideous harshland,
At the witchy hour of gloomness,
All the grobes come oozing home.

You can hear them softly slimeing,
Glissing hissing o'er the slubber,
All those oily boily bodies
Oozing onward in the gloam.

So start to run! Oh, skid and daddle,
Through the slubber slush and sossel!
Skip jump hop and try to skaddle!
All the grobes are on the roam!"

In his study two hundred and forty miles below, the President turned white as the White House. "Jumping jack-rabbits!" he cried. "I think they're after us!"

"Oh, *please* let me blow them up!" said the ex-Chief of the Army.

"Silence!" said Miss Tibbs. "Go stand in the corner!"

In the lobby of the Space Hotel, Mr. Wonka had merely paused in order to think up another verse, and he was just about to start off again when a frightful piercing scream stopped him cold. The screamer was Grandma Josephine. She was sitting up in bed and pointing with a shaking finger at the elevators at the far end of the lobby. She screamed a second time, still pointing, and all eyes turned toward the elevators. The door of the one on the left was sliding slowly open and the watchers could clearly see that there was something . . . something thick . . . something brown . . . something not exactly brown, but greenish-brown . . . something with slimy skin and large eyes . . . squatting inside the elevator!

7
Something Nasty in the Elevators

GRANDMA JOSEPHINE had stopped screaming now. She had gone rigid with shock. The rest of the group by the bed, including Charlie and Grandpa Joe, had become as still as stone. They dared not move. They dared hardly breathe.

And Mr. Wonka, who had swung quickly around to look when the first scream came, was as dumbfounded as the rest. He stood motionless, gaping at the thing in the elevator, his mouth slightly open, his eyes stretched wide as two wheels. What he saw, what they all saw, was this:

It looked more than anything like an enormous egg balanced on its pointed end. It was as tall as a big boy and wider than the fattest man. The greenish-brown skin had a shiny wettish appearance and there were wrinkles in it. About three-quarters up, in the widest part, there were two large round eyes as big as teacups. The eyes were

white, but each had a brilliant red pupil in the center. The red pupils were resting on Mr. Wonka. But now they began traveling slowly across to Charlie and Grandpa Joe and the others by the bed, settling upon them and gazing at them with a cold malevolent stare. The eyes were everything. There were no other features, no nose or mouth or ears, but the entire egg-shaped body was itself moving very, very slightly, pulsing and bulging gently here and there as though the skin were filled with some thick fluid.

At this point, Charlie suddenly noticed that the next elevator was coming down. The indicator numbers above the door were flashing . . . 6 . . . 5 . . . 4 . . . 3 . . . 2 . . . 1 . . . L (for lobby). There was a slight pause. The door slid open, and there, inside the second elevator was another enormous slimy wrinkled greenish-brown egg with eyes.

Now the numbers were flashing above all three of the remaining elevators. Down they came—down, down, down . . . And soon, at precisely the same time, they reached the lobby floor and the doors slid open. Five open doors now . . . one creature in each . . . five in all . . . and five pairs of eyes with brilliant red centers all watching Mr. Wonka and watching Charlie and Grandpa Joe and the others.

There were slight differences in size and shape between the five, but all had the same greenish-brown wrinkled skin and the skin was rippling and pulsing.

For about thirty seconds nothing happened. Nobody stirred, nobody made a sound. The silence was terrible. So was the suspense. Charlie was so frightened he felt himself shrinking inside his skin. Then he saw the creature in the left-hand elevator suddenly starting to change shape! Its body was slowly becoming longer and longer, and thinner and thinner, going up and up toward the roof of the elevator, not straight up, but curving a little to the left, making a snakelike curve that was curiously graceful, up to the left and then curling over the top to the right and coming down again in a half circle; then the bottom end began to grow out as well, like a tail, creeping along the floor . . . creeping along the floor to the left . . . until at last the creature, which had originally looked like a huge egg, now looked like a long curvy serpent standing up on its tail.

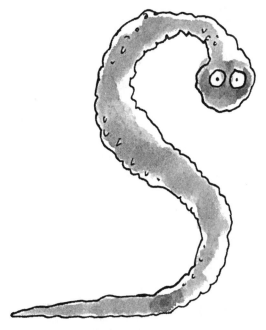

Then the one in the next elevator began stretching itself in much the same way, and what a weird and oozy thing it was to watch! It was twisting itself into a shape that was a bit different from the first, balancing itself almost but not quite on the tip of its tail.

Then the three remaining creatures began stretching themselves all at the same time, each one elongating itself slowly upward, growing taller and taller, thinner and thinner, curving and twisting, stretching and stretching, curling and bending, balancing either on the tail or the head or both, and turned sideways now, so that only one eye was visible. When they had all stopped stretching and bending, this was how they finished up:

"Scram!" shouted Mr. Wonka. "Get out quick!"

People have never moved faster than Grandpa Joe and Charlie and Mr. and Mrs. Bucket at that moment. They all got behind the bed and started pushing like crazy. Mr. Wonka ran in front of them shouting "Scram! Scram! Scram!" And in ten seconds flat all of them were out of the lobby and back inside the Great Glass Elevator. Frantically, Mr. Wonka began undoing bolts and pressing buttons. The door of the Great Glass Elevator snapped shut and the whole thing leaped sideways. They were away! And of course all of them, including the three old ones in the bed, floated up again into the air.

8
The Vermicious Knids

"OH, MY GOODNESS ME!" gasped Mr. Wonka. "Oh, my sainted pants! Oh, my painted ants! Oh, my crawling cats! I hope never to see anything like *that* again!" He floated over to the white button and pressed it. The booster rockets fired. The Elevator shot forward at such a speed that soon the Space Hotel was out of sight far behind.

"But who *were* those awful creatures?" Charlie asked.

"You mean you didn't know?" cried Mr. Wonka. "Well, it's a good thing you didn't. If you'd had even the faintest idea of what horrors you were up against, the marrow would have run out of your bones! You'd have been fossilized with fear and glued to the ground! Then they'd have gotten you! You'd have been a cooked cucumber! You'd have been rasped into a thousand tiny bits, grated like cheese and flocculated alive! They'd have made necklaces from your knucklebones and bracelets from your teeth! Because those creatures, my dear ignorant boy, are the most brutal, vindictive, venemous, murderous beasts in the entire universe!" Here Mr. Wonka paused and ran the tip of a pink tongue all the way around his lips. "VERMICIOUS KNIDS!" he cried. "That's what they were!" He sounded the K . . . K'NIDS, like that.

"I thought they were grobes," Charlie said. "Those oozy-woozy grobes you were telling the President about."

"Oh, no, I just made those up to scare the White House," Mr. Wonka answered. "But there is nothing made up about Vermicious Knids, believe you me. They live, as everybody knows, on the planet Vermes, which is eighteen thousand four hundred and twenty-seven million miles away, and they are very, very clever brutes indeed. The Vermicious Knid can turn itself into any shape it wants. It has no bones. Its body is really one huge muscle, enormously strong, but very stretchy and squishy, like a mixture of rubber and putty with steel wires inside. Normally it is egg-shaped, but it can just as easily give itself two legs like a human, or four legs like a horse. It can become as round as a ball or as long as a kite-string. From fifty yards away, a fully grown Vermicious Knid could stretch out its neck and bite your head off without even getting up!"

"Bite your head off with what?" said Grandma Georgina. "I didn't see any mouth."

"They have other things to bite with," said Mr. Wonka darkly.

"Such as what?" said Grandma Georgina.

"Ring off," said Mr. Wonka. "Your time's up. But listen, everybody. I've just had a funny thought. There I was kidding around with the President and pretending we were creatures from some other planet and by golly, there actually *were* creatures from some other planet on board!"

"Do you think there were many?" Charlie asked. "More than the five we saw?"

"Thousands!" said Mr. Wonka. "There are five hundred rooms in that Space Hotel and there's probably a family of them in every room!"

"Somebody's going to get a nasty shock when they go on board!" said Grandpa Joe.

"They'll be eaten like peanuts," said Mr. Wonka. "Every one of them."

"You don't really mean that, do you, Mr. Wonka?" Charlie said.

"Of course I mean it," said Mr. Wonka. "These Vermicious Knids are the terror of the Universe. They travel through space in great swarms, landing in other stars and planets and destroying everything they find. There used to be some rather nice creatures living on the moon a long time ago. They were called Poozas. But the Vermicious Knids ate the lot. They did the same on Venus and Mars and many other planets."

"Why haven't they come down to our earth and eaten us?" Charlie asked.

"They've tried to, Charlie, many times, but they've never made it. You see, all around our earth there is a vast envelope of air and gas, and anything hitting *that* at high speed gets red-hot. Space capsules are made of special heatproof metal, and when they make a reentry, their speeds are reduced right down to about two thousand miles an hour, first by retro-rockets and then by something called 'friction.' But even so, they get badly scorched. Knids, which are not heatproof at all, and don't have any retro-rockets, get sizzled up completely before they're halfway through. Have you ever seen a shooting star?"

"Lots of them," Charlie said.

"Actually, they're not shooting stars at all," said Mr. Wonka. "They're Shooting Knids. They're Knids trying to enter the earth's atmosphere at high speed and going up in flames."

"What rubbish," said Grandma Georgina.

"You wait," said Mr. Wonka. "You may see it happening before the day is done."

"But if they're so fierce and dangerous," Charlie said, "why didn't they eat us up right away in the Space Hotel? Why did they waste time twisting their bodies into letters and writing SCRAM?"

"Because they're show-offs," Mr. Wonka replied. "They're tremendously proud of being able to write like that."

"But why say SCRAM when they wanted to catch us and eat us?"

"It's the only word they know," Mr. Wonka said.

"*Look!*" screamed Grandma Josephine, pointing through the glass. "Over there!"

Before he even looked, Charlie knew exactly what he was going to see. So did the others. They could tell by the high hysterical note in the old lady's voice.

And there it was, cruising effortlessly alongside them, a simply colossal Vermicious Knid, as thick as a whale, as long as a truck, with the most brutal vermicious look in its eye. It was no more than a dozen yards away, egg-shaped, slimy, greenish brown, with one malevolent red eye (the only one visible) fixed intently upon the people floating inside the Great Glass Elevator.

"The end has come!" screamed Grandma Georgina.

"He'll eat us all!" cried Mrs. Bucket.

"In one gulp," said Mr. Bucket.

"We're done for, Charlie," said Grandpa Joe. Charlie nodded. He couldn't speak or make a sound. His throat was seized up with fright.

But this time Mr. Wonka didn't panic. He remained perfectly calm. "We'll soon get rid of that," he said and he pressed six buttons all at once and six booster rockets went off simultaneously under the Elevator. The Elevator leaped forward like a stung horse, faster and faster, but the great green greasy Knid kept pace alongside it with no trouble at all.

"Make it go away!" yelled Grandma Georgina. "I can't stand it looking at me!"

"Dear lady," said Mr. Wonka, "it can't possibly get in here. I don't mind admitting I was a trifle alarmed back there in the Space Hotel. And with good reason. But here we have nothing to fear. The Great Glass Elevator is shockproof, waterproof, bombproof, bulletproof and Knidproof. So just relax and enjoy it."

"Oh, you Knid, you are vile and vermicious!"
cried Mr. Wonka.

"You are slimy and soggy and squishous!
But what do we care
'Cause you can't get in here,
So hop it and don't get ambitious!"

At this point, the massive Knid outside turned and started cruising away from the Elevator. "There you are!" cried Mr. Wonka, triumphant. "It heard me! It's going home!" But Mr. Wonka was wrong. When the creature was about a hundred yards away, it stopped, hovered for a moment, then went smoothly in reverse, coming back toward the Elevator with its rear-end (which was the pointed end of the egg) now in front. Even going backward, its acceleration was unbelievable. It was like some monstrous bullet coming at them and it came so fast nobody had time even to cry out.

CRASH! It struck the Glass Elevator with the most enormous bang and the whole thing shivered and shook, but the glass held and the Knid bounced off like a rubber ball.

"What did I tell you!" shouted Mr. Wonka, triumphant. "We're safe as sausages in here!"

"He'll have a nasty headache after that," said Grandpa Joe.

"It's not his head, it's his bottom!" said Charlie. "Look Grandpa, there's a big bump coming up on the pointed end where he hit! It's turning black and blue!"

And so it was. A purple bruisy bump the size of a small automobile was appearing on the pointed rear-end of the giant Knid. "Hello, you dirty great beast!" cried Mr. Wonka.

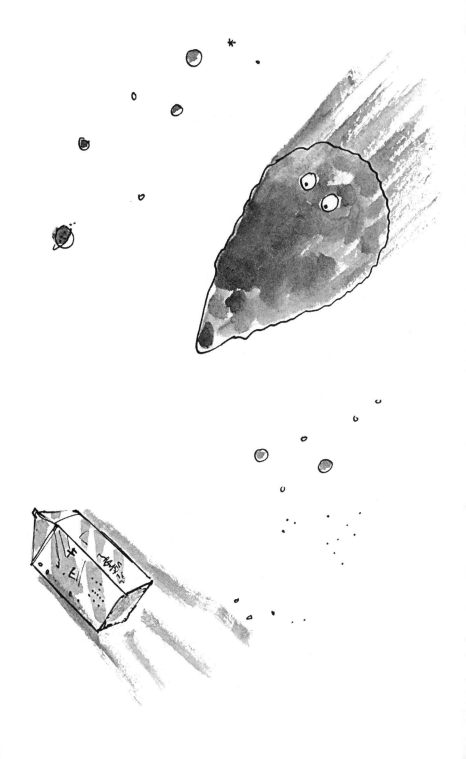

"Hello, you great Knid! Tell us, how do you do?
You're a rather strange color today.
Your bottom is purple and lavender blue.
Should it really be looking that way?

Are you not feeling well? Are you going to faint?
Is it something we cannot discuss?
It must be a very unpleasant complaint,
For your fanny's as big as a bus!

Let me get you a doctor. I know just the man
For a Knid with a nasty disease.
He's a butcher by trade which is not a bad plan,
And he charges quite reasonable fees.

Ah! Here he is now! Doc, you really are kind
To travel so far into space.
There's your patient, the Knid with the
    purple behind!
Do you think it's a desperate case?

'Great heavens above! It's no wonder he's pale!'
Said the doc with a horrible grin.
'There's a sort of balloon on the end of his tail!
I must prick it at once with a pin!'

So he got out a thing like an Indian spear,
With feathers all over the top,
And he lunged and he caught the Knid smack
    in the rear,
But alas, the balloon didn't pop!

Cried the Knid, 'What on earth am I going to do
With this painful preposterous lump?
I can't remain standing the whole summer
      through!
And I cannot sit down on my rump!'

'It's a bad case of rear-ache,' the medico said,
'And it's something I cannot repair.
If you want to sit down, you must sit on
      your head,
With your bottom high up in the air!'"

9

Gobbled Up

————

ON THE DAY when all this was happening, no factories
were open anywhere in the world. All offices and schools
were closed. Nobody moved away from the television
screens, not even for a couple of minutes to get a Coke or
to feed the baby. The tension was unbearable. Everybody
heard the American President's invitation to the men
from Mars to visit him in the White House. And they
heard the weird rhyming reply, which sounded rather
threatening. They also heard a piercing scream (Grandma
Josephine), and a little later on, they heard someone
shouting, "Scram! Scram! Scram!" (Mr. Wonka). Nobody
could make head or tail of the shouting. They took it to

be some kind of Martian language. But when the eight mysterious astronauts suddenly rushed back into their glass capsule and broke away from the Space Hotel, you could almost hear the great sigh of relief that rose up from the peoples of the earth. Telegrams and messages poured into the White House congratulating the President upon his brilliant handling of a frightening situation.

The President himself remained calm and thoughtful. He sat at his desk rolling a small piece of wet chewing gum between his finger and thumb. He was waiting for the moment when he could flick it at Miss Tibbs without her seeing him. He flicked it and missed Miss Tibbs but hit the Secretary of the Interior on the tip of his nose.

"Do you think the men from Mars have accepted my invitation to the White House?" the President asked.

"Of course they have," said the Foreign Secretary. "It was a brilliant speech, sir."

"They're probably on their way down here right now," said Miss Tibbs. "Go and wash that nasty sticky chewing gum off your fingers quickly. They could be here any minute."

"Let's have a song first," said the President. "Please sing another one about me, Nanny."

THE NURSE'S SONG

This mighty man of whom I sing,
The greatest of them all,
Was once a teeny little thing,
Just eighteen inches tall.

I knew him as a tiny tot,
I nursed him on my knee.
I used to sit him on the pot
And wait for him to wee.

I always washed between his toes,
And cut his little nails.
I brushed his hair and wiped his nose
And weighed him on the scales.

Through happy childhood days
  he strayed,
As all nice children should.
I smacked him when he disobeyed,
And stopped when he was good.

It soon began to dawn on me
He wasn't very bright,
Because when he was twenty-three
He couldn't read or write.

'What shall *we do?' his parents sob.*
'The boy has got the vapors!
He couldn't even get a job
Delivering the papers!'

'Ah-ha,' I said, 'this little clot
Could be a politician.'
'Nanny,' he cried, 'Oh Nanny, what
A super proposition!'

'Okay,' I said, 'let's learn and note
The art of politics.
Let's teach you how to miss the boat
And how to drop some bricks,
And how to win the people's vote
And lots of other tricks.

Let's learn to make a speech a day
Upon the T.V. screen,
In which you never never say
Exactly what you mean.
And most important, by the way,
Is not to let your teeth decay,
And keep your fingers clean.'

And now that I am eighty-nine,
It's too late to repent.
The fault was mine the little swine
Became the President.

"Bravo Nanny!" cried the President, clapping his hands. "Hooray!" shouted the others. "Well done, Miss Vice-President, ma'am! Brilliant! Tremendous!"

"My goodness!" said the President. "Those men from Mars will be here any moment! What on earth are we going to give them for lunch? Where's my Chief Cook?"

The Chief Cook was a Frenchman. He was also a French spy and at this moment he was listening at the keyhole of the President's study. *"Ici, Monsieur le President!"* he said, bursting in.

"Chief Cook," said the President. "What do men from Mars eat for lunch?"

"Mars Bars," said the Chief Cook.

"Baked or boiled?" asked the President.

"Oh, *baked*, of course, Monsieur le President. You will ruin a Mars Bar by boiling!"

The voice of astronaut Shuckworth cut in over the

loudspeaker in the President's study. "Request permission to link up and go aboard Space Hotel?" he said.

"Permission granted," said the President. "Go right ahead, Shuckworth. It's all clear now. . . . Thanks to me."

And so the large Commuter Capsule, piloted by Shuckworth, Shanks and Showler, with all the hotel managers and assistant managers and hall porters and pastry chefs and bellhops and waitresses and chambermaids on board, moved in smoothly and linked up with the giant Space Hotel.

"Hey, there! We've lost our television picture," called the President.

"I'm afraid the camera got smashed against the side of the Space Hotel, Mr. President," Shuckworth replied. The President said a very rude word into the microphone and ten million children across the nation began repeating it gleefully and got smacked by their parents.

"All astronauts and one hundred fifty hotel staff safely aboard Space Hotel!" Shuckworth reported over the radio. "We are now standing in the lobby!"

"And what do you think of it all?" asked the President. He knew the whole world was listening in, and he wanted Shuckworth to say how wonderful it was. Shuckworth didn't let him down.

"Gee, Mr. President, it's just *great!*" he said. "It's *unbelievable!* It's so *enormous!* And so . . . it's kind of hard to find words to describe it, it's so truly grand—especially the chandeliers and the carpets and all! I have the Chief Hotel Manager, Mr. Walter W. Wall, beside me now. He would like the honor of a word with you, sir."

"Put him on," said the President.

"Mr. President, sir, this is Walter Wall. What a sumptuous hotel this is! The decorations are superb!"

"Have you noticed that all the carpets are wall to wall, Mr. Walter Wall?" said the President.

"I have indeed, Mr. President."

"All the wallpaper is wall to wall, too, Mr. Walter Wall."

"Yes, sir, Mr. President! Isn't that something! It's going to be a real pleasure running a beautiful hotel like this! *Hey! What's going on over there? Something's coming out of the elevators! Help!*" Suddenly the loudspeaker in the President's study gave out a series of the most ghastly screams and yells. *"Ayeeeee! Owwwww! Ayeeeee! Hel-l-l-lp! Hel-l-l-l-lp! Hel-l-l-l-l-l-l-p!"*

"What on earth's going on?" said the President. *"Shuckworth! Are you there, Shuckworth? . . . Shanks! Showler! Mr. Walter Wall! Where are you all? What's happening?"*

The screams continued. They were so loud the President had to put his fingers in his ears. Every house in the world that had a television or radio receiver heard those awful screams. There were other noises, too. Loud grunts and snortings and crunching sounds. Then there was silence.

Frantically, the President called the Space Hotel on the radio. Houston called the Space Hotel. The President called Houston. Houston called the President. Then both of them called the Space Hotel again. But answer came there none. Up there in space all was silent.

"Something nasty's happened," said the President.

"It's those men from Mars," said the ex-Chief of the Army. "I *told* you to let me blow them up."

"Silence!" snapped the President. "I've got to think."

The loudspeaker began to crackle. "Hello!" it said. "Hello hello hello! Are you receiving me, Space Control in Houston?"

The President grabbed the mike on his desk. "Leave this to me, Houston!" he shouted. "President Gilligrass here, receiving you loud and clear! Go ahead!"

"Astronaut Shuckworth here, Mr. President, back aboard the Commuter Capsule—*thank heavens!*"

"What happened, Shuckworth? Who's with you?"

"We're most of us here, Mr. President, I'm glad to say. Shanks and Showler are with me, and a whole bunch of other folks. I guess we lost maybe a couple of dozen people altogether, pastry chefs, hall porters, that sort of thing. It sure was a scramble getting out of that place alive!"

"What do you mean you *lost* two dozen people?" shouted the President. "How did you lose them?"

"Gobbled up!" replied Shuckworth. "One gulp and that was it! I saw a big six-foot-tall assistant manager being swallowed up just like you'd swallow a lump of ice cream, Mr. President! No chewing—nothing. Just down the hatch!"

"But *who?*" yelled the President. "Who are you talking about? Who did the swallowing?"

"Hold it!" cried Shuckworth. "Oh, my lord, here they all come now! They're coming after us! They're swarming out of the Space Hotel! They're coming out in swarms! You'll have to excuse me a moment, Mr. President. No time to talk right now!"

10
Commuter Capsule in Trouble— Knid Attack Number One

WHILE SHUCKWORTH, Shanks and Showler were being chased out of the Space Hotel by the Knids, Mr. Wonka's Great Glass Elevator was orbiting the earth at tremendous speed. Mr. Wonka had all his booster rockets firing and the Elevator was reaching speeds of thirty-four thousand miles an hour instead of the normal seventeen thousand. They were trying, you see, to get away from that huge angry Vermicious Knid with the purple behind. Mr. Wonka wasn't afraid of it, but Grandma Josephine was petrified. Every time she looked at it, she let out a piercing scream and clapped her hands over her eyes. But of course thirty-four thousand miles an hour is dawdling to a Knid. Healthy young Knids think nothing of traveling a million miles between lunch and supper, and then another million before breakfast the next day. How else could they commute between the plant Vermes and

other stars? Mr. Wonka should have known this and saved his rocket power, but he kept right on going and the giant Knid kept right on cruising effortlessly alongside, glaring into the Elevator with its wicked red eye. "You people have bruised my backside," the Knid seemed to be saying, "and in the end I'm going to get you for that."

They had been streaking around the earth like this for forty-five minutes when Charlie, who was floating comfortably beside Grandpa Joe near the ceiling, said suddenly, "There's something ahead! Can you see it, Grandpa? Straight in front of us!"

"I can, Charlie, I can. . . . Good heavens! It's the Space Hotel!"

"It can't be, Grandpa. We left it miles behind us long ago."

"Ah-ha," said Mr. Wonka. "We've been going so fast we've gone all the way around the earth and caught up with it again. A splendid effort!"

"And there's the Commuter Capsule! Can you see it, Grandpa? It's just behind the Space Hotel!"

"There's something else there, too, Charlie, if I'm not mistaken!"

"I know what those are!" screamed Grandma Josephine. "They're Vermicious Knids! Turn back at once!"

"Reverse!" yelled Grandma Georgina. "Go the other way!"

"Dear lady," said Mr. Wonka. "This isn't an automobile on the highway. When you are in orbit, you cannot stop and you cannot go backward."

"I don't care about that!" shouted Grandma Josephine. "Put on the brakes! Stop! Back-pedal! The Knids'll get us!"

"Now let's for heaven's sake *stop* this nonsense once and for all," Mr. Wonka said sternly. "You know very well my Elevator is completely Knidproof. You have nothing to fear."

They were closer now and they could see the Knids pouring out from the tail of the Space Hotel and swarming like wasps around the Commuter Capsule.

"They're attacking it!" cried Charlie. "They're after the Commuter Capsule!"

It was a fearsome sight. The huge green egg-shape Knids were grouping themselves into squadrons with about twenty Knids to a squadron. Then each squadron formed itself into a line abreast, with one yard between Knids. Then, one after another, the squadrons began attacking the Commuter Capsule. They attacked in reverse with their pointed rear-ends in front and they came in at a fantastic speed.

WHAM! One squadron attacked, bounced off and wheeled away.

CRASH! Another squadron smashed against the side of the Commuter Capsule.

"Get us out of here, you madman!" screamed Grandma Josephine. "What are you waiting for?"

"They'll be coming after *us* next!" yelled Grandma Georgina. "For heaven's sake, man, turn back!"

"I doubt very much if that capsule of theirs is Knidproof," said Mr. Wonka.

"Then we must help them!" cried Charlie. "We've got to do something! There are a hundred and fifty people inside that thing!"

Down on the earth, in the White House study, the President and his advisers were listening in horror to the voices of the astronauts over the radio.

"They're coming at us in droves!" Shuckworth was shouting. "They're bashing us to bits!"

"But *who?*" yelled the president. "You haven't even told us who's attacking you!"

"These dirty great greenish-brown brutes with red eyes!" shouted Shanks, butting in. "They're shaped like enormous eggs and they're coming at us backwards."

"Backwards?" cried the President. "Why backwards?"

"Because their bottoms are even more pointy than

their tops!" shouted Shuckworth. "Look out! Here comes another lot! BANG! We won't be able to stand this much longer, Mr. President! The waitresses are screaming and the chambermaids are all hysterical and the bellhops are being sick and the hall porters are saying their prayers. What shall we do, Mr. President, sir, what on earth shall we do?"

"Fire your rockets, you idiot, and make a reentry!" shouted the President. "Come back to earth immediately!"

"That's impossible!" cried Showler. "They've busted our rockets! They've smashed them to smithereens!"

"We're cooked, Mr. President!" shouted Shanks. "We're done for! Because even if they don't succeed in destroying the capsule, we'll have to stay up here in orbit for the rest of our lives! We can't make a reentry without rockets!"

The President was sweating and the sweat ran all the way down the back of his neck and inside his collar.

"Any moment now, Mr. President," Shanks went on, "we're going to lose contact with you altogether! There's another lot coming at us from the left and they're aiming straight for our radio antenna. Here they come! I don't think we'll be able to . . ." The voice cut. The radio went dead.

"Shanks!" cried the President. "Where are you, Shanks? . . . Shuckworth! Shanks! Showler! . . . Showlworth! Shucks! Shankler! . . . Shankworth! Showl! Shuckler! Why don't you answer me?!"

Up in the Great Glass Elevator where they had no radio and could hear nothing of these conversations, Charlie was saying, "Surely their only hope is to make a reentry and dive back to earth quickly."

"Yes," said Mr. Wonka. "But in order to reenter the earth's atmosphere they've got to kick themselves out of orbit. They've got to change course and head downward and to do that they need rockets! But their rocket tubes are all dented and bent! You can see that from here! They're crippled!"

"Why can't we tow them down?" Charlie asked.

Mr. Wonka jumped. Even though he was floating, he somehow jumped. He was so excited he shot upward and hit his head on the ceiling. Then he spun round three times in the air and cried, "Charlie! You've got it! That's it! We'll tow them out of orbit! To the buttons, quick!"

"What do we tow them with?" asked Grandpa Joe. "Our neckties?"

"Don't you worry about a little thing like that!" cried Mr. Wonka. "My Great Glass Elevator is ready for anything! In we go! Into the breach, dear friends, into the breach!"

"Stop him!" screamed Grandma Josephine.

"You be quiet, Josie," said Grandpa Joe. "There's someone over there needs a helping hand and it's our job to give it. If you're frightened, you'd better just close your eyes tight and stick your fingers in your ears."

11
The Battle of the Knids

"GRANDPA JOE, SIR!" shouted Mr. Wonka. "Kindly jet yourself over to the far corner of the Elevator there and turn that handle! It lowers the rope!"

"A rope's no good, Mr. Wonka! The Knids will bite through a rope in one second!"

"It's a steel rope," said Mr. Wonka. "It's made of reinscorched steel. If they try to bite through *that,* their teeth will splinter like spillikins! To your buttons, Charlie! You've got to help me maneuver. We're going right over the top of the Commuter Capsule and then we'll try to hook onto it somewhere and get a firm hold!"

Like a battleship going into action, the Great Glass Elevator with booster rockets firing moved smoothly in over the top of the enormous Commuter Capsule. The Knids immediately stopped attacking the Capsule and went for the Elevator. Squadron after squadron of giant Vermicious Knids flung themselves furiously against Mr. Wonka's marvelous machine. WHAM! CRASH! BANG! The noise was thunderous and terrible. The Elevator was tossed about the sky like a leaf, and inside it, Grandma Josephine, Grandma Georgina and Grandpa George, floating in their nightshirts, were all yowling and screeching and flapping their arms and calling for help. Mrs. Bucket had wrapped her arms around Mr. Bucket and was clasping him so tightly that one of his shirt buttons punctured his skin. Charlie and Mr. Wonka, as cool as two cantaloupes, were up near the ceiling working the booster-rocket controls, and Grandpa Joe, shouting war cries and throwing curses at the Knids, was down below turning the handle that unwound the steel rope. At the same time, he was watching the rope through the glass floor of the Elevator.

"Starboard a bit, Charlie," shouted Grandpa Joe. "We're right on top of her now! . . . Forward a couple of yards, Mr. Wonka! . . . I'm trying to get the hook hooked around that stumpy thing sticking out in front there! . . . Hold it! . . . I've got it. . . . That's it. . . . Forward a little now and see if it holds! . . . More! . . . More! . . ." The big steel rope tightened. It held! And now, wonder of wonders, with her booster rockets blazing, the Elevator began to tow the huge Commuter Capsule forward and away!

"Full speed ahead!" shouted Grandpa Joe. "She's going to hold! She's holding! She's holding fine!"

"All boosters firing!" cried Mr. Wonka, and the Elevator leaped ahead. Still the rope held. Mr. Wonka jetted himself down to Grandpa Joe and shook him warmly by the hand. "Well done, sir," he said. "You did a brilliant job under heavy fire!"

Charlie looked back at the Commuter Capsule some thirty yards behind them on the end of the tow line. It had little windows up front, and in the windows he could clearly see the flabbergasted faces of Shuckworth, Shanks and Showler. Charlie waved to them and gave them the thumbs-up signal. They didn't wave back. They simply gaped. They couldn't believe what was happening.

Grandpa Joe blew himself upward and hovered beside Charlie, bubbling with excitement. "Charlie, my boy," he said. "We've been through a few funny things together lately, but never anything like this!"

"Grandpa, where are the Knids? They've suddenly vanished."

Everyone looked round. The only Knid in sight was their old friend with the purple behind, still cruising alongside in its usual place, still glaring into the Elevator.

"*Just* a minute!" cried Grandma Josephine. "What's *that* I see over there?" Again they looked, and this time, sure enough, away in the distance, in the deep blue sky of outer space, they saw a massive cloud of Vermicious Knids wheeling and circling like a fleet of bombers.

"If you think we're out of the woods yet, you're crazy!" shouted Grandma Georgina.

"I fear no Knids!" said Mr. Wonka. "We've got them beaten now!"

"Poppyrot and pigwash!" said Grandma Josephine. "Any moment now they'll be at us again! Look at them! They're coming in! They're coming closer!"

This was true. The huge fleet of Knids had moved in at incredible speed and was now flying level with the Great Glass Elevator, a couple of hundred yards away on the right-hand side. The one with the bump on its rear-end was much closer, only twenty yards away on the same side.

"It's changing shape!" cried Charlie. "That nearest one! —what's it going to do? It's getting longer and longer!" And indeed it was. The mammoth egg-shaped body was slowly stretching itself out like chewing gum, becoming longer and longer and thinner and thinner, until in the end it looked exactly like a long slimy-green serpent as thick as a thick tree and as long as a football field. At the front end were the eyes, big and white with red centers, at the back a kind of tapering tail and at the very end of the tail was the enormous round swollen bump it had gotten when it crashed against the glass.

The people floating inside the Elevator watched and waited. Then they saw the long ropelike Knid turning and coming straight but quite slowly toward the Great Glass Elevator. Now it began actually wrapping its ropy body around the Elevator itself. Once around it went . . . then twice around, and very horrifying it was to be inside and to see the soft green body squishing against the outside of the glass no more than a few inches away.

"It's tying us up like a parcel!" yelled Grandma Josephine.

"Bunkum!" said Mr. Wonka.

"It's going to crush us in its coils!" wailed Grandma Georgina.

"Never!" said Mr. Wonka.

Charlie glanced quickly back at the Commuter Capsule. The sheet-white faces of Shuckworth, Shanks and Showler were pressed against the glass of the little windows, terror-struck, stupefied, stunned, their mouths open, their expressions frozen like fishfingers. Once again, Charlie gave them the thumbs-up signal. Showler

acknowledged it with a sickly grin, but that was all.

"Oh, oh, oh!" screamed Grandma Josephine. "Get that beastly squishy thing away from here!"

Having curled its body twice around the Elevator, the Knid now proceeded to tie a knot with its two ends, a good strong knot, left over right, then right over left. When it had pulled the knot tight, there remained about five yards of one end hanging loose. This was the end with the eyes on it. But it didn't hang loose for long. It quickly curled itself into the shape of a huge hook and the hook stuck straight out sideways from the Elevator as though waiting for something else to hook itself onto it.

While all this was going on, nobody had noticed what the other Knids were up to. "Mr. Wonka!" Charlie cried. "Look at the others! What *are* they doing?"

What indeed?

These, too, had all changed shape and had become longer, but not nearly so long or so thin as the first one. Each of them had turned itself into a kind of thick rod and the rod was curled around at both ends—at the tail end and at the head end—so that it made a double-ended hook. And now all the hooks were linking up into one long chain—one thousand Knids, all joining together and curving around in the sky to make a chain of Knids half a mile long or more! And the Knid at the very front of the chain (whose front hook was not, of course, hooked up to anything) was leading them in a wide circle and sweeping in toward the Great Glass Elevator.

"Hey!" shouted Grandpa Joe. "They're going to hook up with this brute who's tied himself around us!"

"And tow us away!" cried Charlie.

"To the planet Vermes," gasped Grandma Josephine. "Eighteen thousand four hundred and twenty-seven million miles from here!"

"They can't do that!" cried Mr. Wonka. "*We're* doing the towing around here!"

"They're going to link up, Mr. Wonka!" Charlie said. "They really are! Can't we stop them? They're going to tow us away and they're going to tow the people we're towing away as well!"

"Do something, you old fool!" shrieked Grandma Georgina. "Don't just float about looking at them!"

"I must admit," said Mr. Wonka, "that for the first time in my life I find myself at a bit of a loss."

They all stared in horror through the glass at the long chain of Vermicious Knids. The leader of the chain was coming closer and closer. The hook, with two big angry eyes on it, was out and ready. In thirty seconds it would link up with the hook of the Knid wrapped around the Elevator.

"I want to go home!" wailed Grandma Josephine. "Why can't we all go home?"

"Great thundering tomcats!" cried Mr. Wonka. "*Home* is right! What on earth am I thinking of! Come on, Charlie! Quick! REENTRY! You take the yellow button! Press it for all you're worth! I'll handle this lot!" Charlie and Mr. Wonka literally flew to the buttons. "Hold your hats!" shouted Mr. Wonka. "Grab your gizzards! We're going down!"

Rockets started firing out of the Elevator from all sides. It tilted and gave a sickening lurch and then plunged downward into the earth's atmosphere at a simply colossal speed. *Retro-rockets!* bellowed Mr. Wonka.

"I mustn't forget to fire the retro-rockets!" He flew over to another series of buttons and started playing on them like a piano.

The Elevator was now streaking downward head first, upside down, and all the passengers found themselves floating upside down as well.

"Help!" screamed Grandma Georgina. "All the blood's going to my head!"

"Then turn yourself the other way up," said Mr. Wonka. "That's easy enough, isn't it?"

Everyone blew and puffed and turned somersaults in the air until at last they were all the right way up. "How's the tow rope holding, Grandpa?" Mr. Wonka called out.

"They're still with us, Mr. Wonka, sir! The rope's holding fine."

It was an amazing sight—The Great Elevator streaking down toward the earth with the huge Commuter Capsule in tow behind it. But the long chain of Knids was coming after them, following them down, keeping pace with them easily, and now the hook of the leading Knid in the chain was actually reaching out and grasping for the hook made by the Knid on the Elevator.

"We're too late!" screamed Grandma Georgina. "They're going to link up and haul us back!"

"I think not," said Mr. Wonka. "Don't you remember what happens when a Knid enters the earth's atmosphere at high speed? He gets red-hot. He burns away in a long fiery trail. He becomes a Shooting Knid. Soon these dirty beasts will start popping like popcorn!"

As they streaked on downward, sparks began to fly off the sides of the Elevator. The glass glowed pink, then red, then scarlet. Sparks also began to fly off the long chain of Knids, and the leading Knid in the chain started to shine like a red-hot poker. So did all the others. So did the great slimy brute coiled around the Elevator itself. This one, in fact, was trying frantically to uncoil itself and get away, but it was having trouble untying the knot, and in another ten seconds it began to sizzle. Inside the Elevator they could actually hear the sizzling. It made a noise like bacon frying. And exactly the same sort of thing was happening to the other one thousand Knids in the chain. The tremendous heat was simply sizzling them up. They were red-hot, every one of them. Then suddenly, they became white-hot and they gave out a dazzling white light.

"They're shooting Knids!" cried Charlie.

"What a splendid sight," said Mr. Wonka. "It's better than fireworks."

In a few seconds more, the Knids had blown away in a cloud of ashes and it was all over. "We've done it!" cried Mr. Wonka. "They've been roasted to a crisp! They've been frizzled to a fritter! We're saved!"

"What do you mean saved?" said Grandma Josephine. "We'll all be frizzled ourselves if this goes on any longer! We'll be barbecued like beefsteaks! Look at that glass! It's hotter than a fizzgig!"

"Have no fears, dear lady," answered Mr. Wonka. "My Elevator is air-conditioned, ventilated, aerated and automated in every possible way. We're going to be all right now."

"I haven't the faintest idea what's been going on," said Mrs. Bucket, making one of her rare speeches. "But whatever it is, I don't like it."

"Aren't you enjoying it, Mother?" Charlie asked her.

"No," she said. "I'm not. Nor is your father."

"What a great sight it is!" said Mr. Wonka. "Just look at the earth down there, Charlie, getting bigger and bigger!"

"And us going to meet it at two thousand miles an hour!" groaned Grandma Georgina. "How are you going to slow down for heaven's sake? You didn't think of that, did you?"

"He's got parachutes," Charlie told her. "I'll bet he's got great big parachutes that open just before we hit."

"Parachutes!" said Mr. Wonka with contempt. "Parachutes are only for astronauts and sissies! And anyway, we don't want to *slow down*. We want to *speed up*. I've told you already we've got to be going at an absolutely tremendous speed when we hit. Otherwise, we'll never punch our way in through the roof of the Chocolate Factory."

"How about the Commuter Capsule?" Charlie asked anxiously.

"We'll be letting them go in a few seconds now," Mr. Wonka answered. "They *do* have parachutes, three of them, to slow them down on the last bit."

"How do you know we won't land in the Pacific Ocean?" said Grandma Josephine.

"I don't," said Mr. Wonka. "But we all know how to swim, do we not?"

"This man," shouted Grandma Josephine, "is crazy as a crumpet!"

"He's cracked as a crawfish!" cried Grandma Georgina.

Down and down plunged the Great Glass Elevator. Nearer and nearer came the earth below. Oceans and continents rushed up to meet them, getting bigger every second. . . .

"Grandpa Joe, sir! Throw out the rope! Let it go," ordered Mr. Wonka. "They'll be all right now so long as their parachutes are working."

"Rope gone!" called out Grandpa Joe, and the huge Commuter Capsule, on its own now, began to swing away to one side. Charlie waved to the three astronauts in the front window. None of them waved back. They were still sitting there in a kind of shocked daze, gaping at the old ladies and the old men and the small boy floating about in the Glass Elevator.

"It won't be long now," said Mr. Wonka, reaching for a row of tiny pale blue buttons in one corner. "We shall soon know whether we are alive or dead. Keep very quiet please for this final part. I have to concentrate awfully hard, otherwise we'll come down in the wrong place."

They plunged into a thick bank of clouds and for ten seconds they could see nothing. When they came out of the clouds, the Commuter Capsule had disappeared, and the earth was very close, and there was only a great spread of land beneath them with mountains and forests . . . then fields and trees . . . then a small town.

"There it is!" shouted Mr. Wonka. "My Chocolate Factory! My beloved Chocolate Factory!"

"You mean *Charlie's* Chocolate Factory," said Grandpa Joe.

"That's *right!*" said Mr. Wonka, addressing Charlie. "I'd clean forgotten! I do apologize to you my dear boy! Of course it's yours! And here we go!"

Through the glass floor of the Elevator, Charlie caught a quick glimpse of the huge red roof and the tall chimneys of the giant factory. They were plunging straight down onto it.

"Hold your breath!" shouted Mr. Wonka. "Hold your nose! Fasten your seat belts and say your prayers! We're going through the roof!"

12
Back to the Chocolate Factory

AND THEN THE NOISE of splintering wood and broken glass and absolute darkness and the most awful crunching sounds as the Elevator rushed on and on, smashing everything before it.

All at once, the crashing noises stopped and the ride became smoother and the Elevator seemed to be traveling on guides or rails, twisting and turning like a roller coaster.

And when the lights came on, Charlie suddenly realized that for the last few seconds he hadn't been floating at all. He had been standing normally on the floor. Mr. Wonka was on the floor, too, and so was Grandpa Joe and Mr. and Mrs. Bucket, and also the big bed. As for Grandma Josephine, Grandma Georgina and Grandpa George, they must have fallen right back onto the bed because they were now all three on top of it and scrabbling to get under the blanket.

"We're through!" yelled Mr. Wonka. "We've done it! We're in!" Grandpa Joe grabbed him by the hand and said, "Well done, sir! How splendid! What a magnificent job!"

"Where in the world are we now?" said Mrs. Bucket.

"We're back, Mother!" Charlie cried. "We're in the Chocolate Factory!"

"I'm very glad to hear it," said Mrs. Bucket. "But didn't we come rather a long way round?"

"We had to," said Mr. Wonka, "to avoid the traffic."

"I have never met a man," said Grandma Georgina, "who talks so much absolute nonsense!"

"A little nonsense now and then, is relished by the wisest men," Mr. Wonka said.

"Why don't you pay some attention to where this crazy elevator's going!" shouted Grandma Josephine. "And stop footling about!"

"A little footling round about, will stop you going up the spout," said Mr. Wonka.

"What did I tell you!" cried Grandma Georgina. "He's round the twist! He's bogged as a beetle! He's dotty as a dingbat! He's got rats in the roof! I want to go home!"

"Too late," said Mr. Wonka. "We're there!" The Elevator stopped. The doors opened and Charlie found himself looking out once again at the great Chocolate Room with the chocolate river and the chocolate waterfall, where everything was eatable—the trees, the leaves, the grass, the pebbles and even the rocks. And there to meet them were hundreds and hundreds of tiny Oompa-Loompas, all waving and cheering. It was a sight that took one's breath away. Even Grandma Georgina was stunned into silence for a few seconds. But not for long.

"Who in the world are all those peculiar little men?" she said.

"They're Oompa-Loompas," Charlie told her. "They're wonderful. You'll love them."

"Ssshh," said Grandpa Joe. "Listen, Charlie. The drums are starting up. They're going to sing."

"Alleluia!" sang the Oompa-Loompas.
"Oh alleluia and hooray!

Our Willy Wonka's back today!
We thought you'd never make it home!
We thought you'd left us all alone!
We knew that you would have to face
Some frightful creatures up in space.
We even thought we heard the crunch
Of someone eating you for lunch ..."

"All right!" shouted Mr. Wonka, laughing and raising both hands. "Thank you for your welcome. Will some of you please help to get this bed out of here?"

Fifty Oompa-Loompas ran forward and pushed the bed with the three old ones in it out of the elevator. Mr. and Mrs. Bucket, both looking completely overwhelmed by it all, followed the bed out. Then came Grandpa Joe, Charlie and Mr. Wonka.

"Now," said Mr. Wonka, addressing Grandpa George, Grandma Georgina and Grandma Josephine. "Up you hop out of that bed and let's get cracking. I'm sure you'll all want to lend a hand running the factory."

"Who, us?" said Grandma Josephine.

"Yes, you," said Mr. Wonka.

"You must be joking," said Grandma Georgina.

"I never joke," said Mr. Wonka.

"Now just you listen to me, sir," said old Grandpa George, sitting up straight in bed. "You've gotten us into quite enough tubbles and trumbles for one day!"

"I've gotten you out of them, too," said Mr. Wonka proudly. "And I'm going to get you out of that bed as well, you see if I don't!"

13
How Wonka-Vite Was Invented

"I HAVEN'T BEEN out of this bed in twenty years and I'm not getting out now for anybody," said Grandma Josephine firmly.

"Nor me," said Grandma Georgina.

"You were out of it just now, every one of you," said Mr. Wonka.

"That was floating," said Grandpa George. "We couldn't help it."

"We never put our feet on the floor," said Grandma Josephine.

"Try it," said Mr. Wonka. "You might surprise yourself."

"Go on, Josie," said Grandpa Joe. "Give it a try. I did. It was easy."

"We're perfectly comfortable where we are, thank you very much," said Grandma Josephine.

Mr. Wonka sighed and shook his head very slowly and very sadly. "Oh well," he said, "so that's that." He laid his head on one side and gazed thoughtfully at the three old people in the bed, and Charlie, watching him closely, saw those bright little eyes of his beginning to spark and twinkle once again.

Ha-Ha, thought Charlie. What's coming now?

"I suppose," said Mr. Wonka, placing the tip of one finger on the point of his nose and pressing gently, "I suppose, because this is a very special case . . . I suppose

I *could* spare you just a tiny little bit of . . ." He stopped
and shook his head.

"A tiny little bit of what?" said Grandma Josephine
sharply.

"No," said Mr. Wonka. "It's pointless. You seem to have
decided to stay in that bed no matter what happens. And
anyway, the stuff is much too precious to waste. I'm sorry
I mentioned it." He started to walk away.

"Hey!" shouted Grandma Georgina. "You can't start
something and not go on with it! *What* is too precious to
waste?"

Mr. Wonka stopped. Slowly he turned around. He
looked long and hard at the three old people in the bed.
They looked back at him, waiting. He kept silent a little
longer, allowing their curiosity to grow. The Oompa-
Loompas stood absolutely still behind him, watching.

"What is this thing you're talking about?" said Grandma Georgina.

"Get on with it, for heaven's sake!" said Grandma Josephine.

"Very well," Mr. Wonka said at last. "I'll tell you. And listen carefully because this could change your whole lives. It could even change *you.*"

"I don't want to be *changed!*" shouted Grandma Georgina.

"May I go on, madam? Thank you. Not long ago, I was fooling about in my Inventing Room, stirring stuff around and mixing things up the way I do every afternoon at four o'clock, when suddenly I found I had made something that seemed very unusual. This thing I had made kept changing color as I looked at it, and now and again it gave a little jump, it actually jumped up in the air, as though it were alive. 'What have we here?' I cried, and I rushed it quickly to the Testing Room and gave some to the Oompa-Loompa who was on duty there at the time. The result was immediate! It was flabbergasting! It was unbelievable! It was also rather unfortunate."

"What happened?" said Grandma Georgina, sitting up.

"What indeed," said Mr. Wonka.

"Answer her question," said Grandma Josephine. "What happened to the Oompa-Loompa?"

"Ah," said Mr. Wonka. "Yes . . . well . . . there's no point in crying over spilled milk, is there? I realized, you see, that I had stumbled upon a new and tremendously powerful vitamin, and I also knew that if only I could make it safe, if only I could stop it doing to others what it did to that Oompa-Loompa . . ."

"What *did* it do to that Oompa-Loompa?" said Grandma Georgina sternly.

"The older I get, the deafer I become," said Mr. Wonka. "Do please raise your voice a trifle next time. Thank you so much. Now then. I simply *had* to find a way of making this stuff safe, so that people could take it without, er . . ."

"Without *what?*" snapped Grandma Georgina.

"Without a leg to stand on," said Mr. Wonka. "So I rolled up my sleeves and set to work once more in the Inventing Room. I mixed and I mixed. I must have tried just about every mixture under the moon. By the way, there is a little hole in one wall of the Inventing Room which connects directly with the Testing Room next door, so I was always able to keep passing stuff through for testing to whichever brave volunteer happened to be on duty. Well, the first few weeks were pretty depressing and we won't talk about them. Instead, let me tell you what happened on the one hundred and thirty-second day of my labors. That morning, I had changed the mixture drastically, and this time the little pill I produced at the end of it all was not nearly so active or alive as the others had been. It kept changing color, yes, but only from lemon yellow to blue, then back to yellow again. And when I placed it on the palm of my hand, it didn't jump about like a grasshopper. It only quivered, and then ever so slightly.

"I ran to the hole in the wall that led to the Testing Room. A very old Oompa-Loompa was on duty there that morning. He was a bald, wrinkled, toothless old fellow. He was in a wheelchair. He had been in the wheelchair for at least fifteen years.

"'This is test number one hundred and thirty-two!' I said, chalking it up on the board.

"I handed him the pill. He looked at it nervously. I couldn't blame him for being a bit jittery after what had happened to the other one hundred and thirty-one volunteers."

"What *had* happened to them?" shouted Grandma Georgina. "Why don't you answer the question instead of skidding around it on two wheels?"

"Who knows the way out of a rose?" said Mr. Wonka. "So this brave old Oompa-Loompa took the pill and with the help of a little water, he gulped it down. Suddenly, the most amazing thing happened. Before my very eyes, queer little changes began taking place in the way he looked. A moment earlier, he had been practically bald,

with just a fringe of snowy white hair around the sides and the back of his head. But now the fringe of white hair was turning gold and all over the top of his head new gold hair was beginning to sprout, like grass. In less than half a minute, he had grown a splendid new crop of long golden hair. At the same time, many of the wrinkles started disappearing from his face, not all of them, but about half, enough to make him look a good deal younger, and all of this must have given him a nice tickly feeling because he started grinning at me, then laughing, and as soon as he opened his mouth, I saw the strangest sight of all. Teeth were growing up out from those old toothless gums, good white teeth, and they were coming up so fast I could actually see them getting bigger and bigger.

"I was too flabbergasted to speak. I just stood there with my head poking through the hole in the wall, staring at the little Oompa-Loompa. I saw him slowly lifting himself out of his wheelchair. He tested his legs on the ground. He stood up. He walked a few paces. Then he looked up at me and his face was bright. His eyes were huge and bright as two stars.

"'Look at me,' he said softly. 'I'm walking! It's a miracle!'

"'It's Wonka-Vite!' I said. 'The great rejuvenator! It makes you young again. How old do you feel now?'

"He thought very carefully about this question, then he said, 'I feel almost exactly how I felt when I was fifty years old.'

"'How old were you just now, before you took the Wonka-Vite?' I asked him.

"'Seventy last birthday,' he answered.

"'That means,' I said, 'it has made you twenty years younger.'

"'It has, it has!' he cried, delighted. 'I feel as frisky as a froghopper!'

"'Not frisky enough,' I told him. 'Fifty is still pretty old. Let us see if I can't help you a bit more. Stay right where you are. I'll be back in a twink.'

"I ran to my workbench and quickly made one more pill of Wonka-Vite, using exactly the same mixture as before.

"'Swallow this,' I said, passing the second pill through the hatch. There was no hesitating this time. Eagerly, he popped it into his mouth and chased it down with a drink of water. And behold, within half a minute, another twenty years had fallen away from his face and body and he was now a slim and sprightly young Oompa-Loompa of thirty. He gave a whoop of joy and started dancing around the room, leaping high in the air and coming down on his toes. 'Are you happy?' I asked him.

"'I'm ecstatic!' he cried, jumping up and down. 'I'm happy as a horse in a hayfield!' He ran out of the Testing Room to show himself off to his family and friends.

"Thus was Wonka-Vite invented," said Mr. Wonka. "And thus was it made safe for all to use."

"Why don't you use it yourself, then?" said Grandma Georgina. "You told Charlie you were getting too old to run the factory, so why don't you just take a couple of pills and get forty years younger? Tell me that?"

"Anyone can ask questions," said Mr. Wonka. "It's the answers that count. Now then, if the three of you in the bed would care to try a dose . . ."

"Just one minute!" said Grandma Josephine, sitting up straight. "First I'd like to take a look at this seventy-year-old Oompa-Loompa who is now back to thirty."

Mr. Wonka flicked his fingers. A tiny Oompa-Loompa, looking young and perky, ran forward out of the crowd and did a marvelous little dance in front of the three old people in the big bed. "Two weeks ago, he was seventy years old and in a wheelchair," Mr. Wonka said proudly. "And look at him now!"

"The drums, Charlie!" said Grandpa Joe. "Listen! They're starting up again!"

Far away down on the bank of the chocolate river, Charlie could see the Oompa-Loompa band striking up once more. There were twenty Oompa-Loompas in the band, each with an enormous drum twice as tall as himself, and they were beating a slow mysterious rhythm that soon had all the other hundreds of Oompa-Loompas swinging and swaying from side to side in a kind of trance. They began to chant:

> *"If you are old and have the shakes,*
> *If all your bones are full of aches,*
> *If you can hardly walk at all,*
> *If living drives you up the wall*
> *If you're a grump and full of spite,*
> *If you're a human parasite,*
> *Then what you need is Wonka-Vite!*
> *Your eyes will shine, your hair will grow,*
> *Your face and skin will start to glow.*
> *Your rotten teeth will all drop out*

And in their place new teeth will sprout.
Those rolls of fat around your hips
Will vanish, and your wrinkled lips
Will get so soft and rosy pink
That all the boys will smile and wink
And whisper secretly that this
Is just the girl they want to kiss!
But wait! For that is not the most
Important thing of which to boast.
Good looks you'll have, we've told you so,
But looks aren't everything, you know.
Each pill, as well, to you will give
An extra twenty years to live!
So come, old friends, and do what's right!
Let's make your lives as bright as bright!
Let's take a dose of this delight!
This heavenly magic dynamite!
You can't go wrong, you must go right!
It's Willy Wonka's Wonka-Vite!"

14
Recipe for Wonka-Vite

"HERE IT IS!" cried Mr. Wonka, standing at the end of the bed and holding high in one hand a little bottle. "The most valuable bottle of pills in the world! And that, by the way," he said, giving Grandma Georgina a saucy glance, "is

why I haven't taken any myself. They are far too valuable
to waste on me."

He held the bottle out over the bed. The three old ones
sat up and stretched their scrawny necks, trying to catch
a glimpse of the pills inside. Charlie and Grandpa Joe also
came forward to look. So did Mr. and Mrs. Bucket. The
label said:

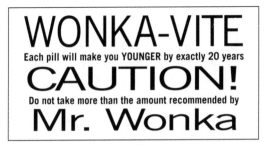

They could all see the pills through the glass. They were a brilliant yellow, shimmering and quivering inside the bottle. Vibrating is perhaps a better word. They were vibrating so rapidly that each pill became a blur and you couldn't see its shape. You could see only its color. You got the impression that there was something very small but incredibly powerful, something not quite of this world, locked up inside them and fighting to get out.

"They're wriggling," said Grandma Georgina. "I don't like things that wriggle. How do we know they won't go on wriggling inside us after we've swallowed them? Like those Mexican jumping beans of Charlie's I swallowed a couple of years back. You remember that, Charlie?"

"I told you not to eat them, Grandma."

"They went on jumping about inside me for a month," said Grandma Georgina. "I couldn't sit still."

"If I'm going to eat one of those pills, I sure as heck want to know what's in it first," said Grandma Josephine.

"I don't blame you," said Mr. Wonka. "But the recipe is extremely complicated. Wait a minute. I've got it written down somewhere . . ." He started digging around in the pockets of his coattails. "I know it's here somewhere," he said. "I couldn't have lost it. I keep all my most valuable and important things in these pockets. The trouble is, there's such a lot of them . . ." He started emptying the pockets and placing the contents on the bed—a home-made catapult, a Yo-Yo, a trick fried egg made of rubber, a slice of salami, a tooth with a filling in it, a stinkbomb, a packet of itching powder . . . "It must be here, it must be, it *must*," he kept muttering. "I put it away so carefully. . . . Ah! *Here* it is!" He unfolded a crumpled piece of paper, smoothed it out, held it up, and began to read as follows:

RECIPE FOR MAKING WONKA-VITE

Take a block of finest chocolate weighing one ton (or twenty sackfuls of broken chocolate, whichever is the easier). Place chocolate in very large cauldron and melt over red-hot furnace. When melted, lower heat slightly so as not to burn the chocolate, but keep it boiling. Now add the following, in precisely the order given, stirring well all the time and allowing each item to dissolve before adding the next:

THE HOOF OF A MANTICORE

THE TRUNK (AND THE SUITCASE) OF AN ELEPHANT

THE YOLKS OF THREE EGGS FROM A WHIFFLEBIRD

A WART FROM A WART HOG

THE HORN OF A COW (IT MUST BE A LOUD HORN)

THE FRONT TAIL OF A COCKATRICE

SIX OUNCES OF SPRUNGE FROM A YOUNG SLIMESCRAPER

TWO HAIRS (AND ONE RABBIT) FROM THE HEAD OF A

    HIPPOCAMPUS

THE BEAK OF A RED-BREASTED WILBATROSS

A CORN FROM THE TOE OF A UNIHORN

THE FOUR TENTACLES OF A QUADROPUS

THE HIP (AND THE PO AND THE POT) OF A HIPPOPOTAMUS

THE SNOUT OF A PROGHOPPER

A MOLE FROM A MOLE

THE HIDE (AND THE SEEK) OF A SPOTTED WHANGDOODLE

THE WHITES OF TWELVE EGGS FROM A TREESQUEAK

THE THREE FEET OF A SNOZZWANGER (IF YOU CAN'T
   GET THREE FEET, ONE YARD WILL DO)
THE SQUARE ROOT OF A SOUTH AMERICAN ABACUS
THE FANGS OF A VIPER (IT MUST BE A VINDSHIELD
   VIPER)
THE CHEST (AND THE DRAWERS) OF A WILD GROUT

When all the above are thoroughly dissolved, boil for a further twenty-seven days but do not stir. At the end of this time, all liquid will have evaporated and there will be left in the bottom of the cauldron only a hard brown lump about the size of a football. Break this open with a hammer and in the very center of it you will find a small round pill. This pill is WONKA-VITE.

15
Good-Bye, Georgina

WHEN MR. WONKA had finished reading the recipe, he carefully folded the paper and put it back into his pocket. "A very, *very* complicated mixture," he said. "So can you wonder it took me so long to get it just right?" He held the bottle up high and gave it a little shake and the pills rattled loudly inside it, like glass beads. "Now, sir," he said, offering the bottle first to Grandpa George. "Will you take one pill or two?"

"Will you solemnly swear," said Grandpa George, "that

it will do what you say it will and nothing else?"

Mr. Wonka placed his free hand on his heart. "I swear it," he said.

Charlie edged forward. Grandpa Joe came with him. The two of them always stayed close together. "Please excuse me for asking," Charlie said, "but are you really absolutely sure you've got it *quite right?*"

"Whatever makes you ask a funny question like that?" said Mr. Wonka.

"I was thinking of the gum you gave to Violet Beauregarde," Charlie said.

"So *that's* what's bothering you!" cried Mr. Wonka. "But don't you understand, my dear boy, that I never *did* give that gum to Violet? She snatched it without permission. And I shouted, 'Stop! Don't! Spit it out!' But the silly girl took no notice of me. Now Wonka-Vite is altogether different. I am *offering* these pills to your grandparents. I am *recommending* them. And when taken according to my instructions, they are as safe as sugar candy!"

"Of course they are!" cried Mr. Bucket. "What are you waiting for, all of you?"

An extraordinary change had come over Mr. Bucket since he had entered the Chocolate Room. Normally, he was a pretty timid sort of person. A lifetime devoted to screwing caps onto the tops of toothpaste tubes in a toothpaste factory had turned him into a rather shy and quiet man. But the sight of the marvelous Chocolate Factory had made his spirit soar. What is more, this business of the pills seemed to have given him a terrific kick. "Listen!" he cried, going up to the edge of the bed. "Mr. Wonka's offering you a new life! Grab it while you can!"

"It's a delicious sensation," Mr. Wonka said. "And it's very quick. You will lose a year a second. Exactly one year falls away from you every second that goes by." He stepped forward and placed the bottle of pills gently in the middle of the bed. "So here you are, my dears," he said. "Help yourselves!"

"Come on!" cried all the Oompa-Loompas together.
"Come on, old friends, and do what's right!
Come make your lives as bright as bright!
Just take a dose of this delight!
This heavenly magic dynamite!
You can't go wrong, you must go right!
IT'S WILLY WONKA'S WONKA-VITE!"

This was too much for the old people in the bed. All three of them made a dive for the bottle. Six scrawny hands shot out and started scrabbling to get hold of it. Grandma Georgina got it. She gave a grunt of triumph and unscrewed the cap and tipped all the little brilliant yellow pills onto the blanket on her lap. She cupped her hands around them so the others couldn't reach out and snatch them. "All right!" she shouted excitedly, counting them quickly. "There's twelve pills here. That's six for me and three for each of you!"

"Hey! That's not fair!" shrilled Grandma Josephine. "It's four for each of us!"

"Four each is right!" cried Grandpa George. "Come on, Georgina! Hand over my share!"

Mr. Wonka shrugged his shoulders and turned his back on them. He hated squabbles. He hated it when people got grabby and selfish. Let them fight it out among themselves, he thought, and he walked away. He walked slowly down toward the chocolate waterfall. It was an unhappy truth, he told himself, that nearly all people in the world behave badly when there is something really big at stake. Money is the thing they fight over most. But these pills were bigger than money. They could do things for you no amount of money could ever do. They were worth at least a million dollars a pill. He knew plenty of very rich men who would gladly pay that much in order to become twenty years younger. He reached the riverbank below the waterfall and he stood there gazing at the great gush and splash of melted chocolate pouring down. He had hoped the noise of the waterfall would drown the arguing voices of the old grandparents in the bed, but it didn't. Even with his back to them, he still couldn't help hearing most of what they were saying.

"I had them first!" Grandma Georgina was shouting. "So they're mine to hand out!"

"Oh no they're not!" shrilled Grandma Josephine. "He didn't give them to you! He gave them to all three of us!"

"I want my share and no one's going to stop me getting it!" yelled Grandpa George. "Come on, woman! Hand them over!"

Then came the voice of Grandpa Joe, cutting in sternly through the rabble. "Stop this at once!" he ordered. "All three of you! You're behaving like savages!"

"You keep out of this, Joe, and mind your own business!" said Grandma Josephine.

"Now you be careful, Josie," Grandpa Joe went on. "Four is too many for one person anyway."

"That's right," Charlie said. "*Please,* Grandma, why don't you just take one or two each, like Mr. Wonka said, and that'll leave some for Grandpa Joe and mother and father."

"Yes!" cried Mr. Bucket. "I'd love one."

"Oh, wouldn't it be wonderful," said Mrs. Bucket, "to be twenty years younger and not have aching feet anymore! Couldn't you spare just one for each of us, Mother?"

"I'm afraid not," said Grandma Georgina. "These pills are especially reserved for us three in the bed. Mr. Wonka said so."

"I want my share!" shouted Grandpa George. "Come on, Georgina! Dish them out!"

"Hey, let me go, you brute!" cried Grandma Georgina. "You're hurting me! Ow! . . . All right! *All right!* I'll share them if you'll stop twisting my arm. . . . That's better. . . . Here's four for Josephine . . . four for George . . . and four for me."

"Good," said Grandpa George. "Now who's got some water?"

Without looking around, Mr. Wonka knew that three Oompa-Loompas would be running to the bed with three glasses of water. Oompa-Loompas were always ready to help. There was a brief pause, and then:

"Well, here goes!" cried Grandpa George.

"Young and beautiful, that's what I'll be!" shouted Grandma Josephine.

"Farewell, old age!" cried Grandma Georgina. "All together now! Down the hatch!"

Then there was silence. Mr. Wonka was itching to turn

around and look, but he forced himself to wait. Out of the corner of one eye he could see a group of Oompa-Loompas, all motionless, their eyes fixed intently in the direction of the big bed over by the elevator. Then Charlie's voice broke the silence. *"Wow!"* he was shouting. "Just look at *that!* That's fantastic! It's . . . it's incredible!"

"I can't believe it!" Grandpa Joe was yelling. "They're getting younger and younger! They really are! Just *look* at Grandpa George's hair!"

"And his teeth!" cried Charlie. "Hey, Grandpa! You're getting lovely white teeth all over again!"

"Mother!" shouted Mrs. Bucket to Grandma Georgina. "Oh, Mother! You're beautiful! You're so young! And just *look* at Dad!" she went on, pointing at Grandpa George. "Isn't he the handsomest thing?"

"What's it feel like, Josie?" asked Grandpa Joe excitedly. "Tell us what it feels like to be back to thirty again! . . . Wait a minute! You look younger than thirty! You can't be a day more than twenty now! . . . But that's enough, isn't it? . . . I would stop there if I were you. Twenty's quite young enough!"

Mr. Wonka shook his head sadly and passed a hand over his eyes. Had you been standing very close to him you would have heard him murmuring softly under his breath, "Oh, deary deary me, here we go again . . ."

"Mother!" cried Mrs. Bucket, and now there was a shrill note of alarm in her voice. "Why don't you stop, Mother? You're going too far! You're way under twenty! You can't be more than fifteen! You're . . . you're . . . you're ten! *You're getting smaller, Mother!"*

"Josie!" shouted Grandpa Joe. "Hey, Josie! Don't do it, Josie! You're shrinking! You're a little girl! Stop her, somebody! Quick!"

"They're *all* going too far!" cried Charlie.

"They took too much," said Mr. Bucket.

"Mother's shrinking faster than any of them," wailed Mrs. Bucket. *"Mother! Can't you hear me, Mother? Can't you stop?"*

"My heavens, isn't it quick!" said Mr. Bucket, who seemed to be the only one enjoying it. "It really is a year a second!"

"But they've hardly got any more years left!" wailed Grandpa Joe.

"Mother's no more than four now," Mrs. Bucket cried out. "She's three . . . two . . . one . . . *Gracious me!* What's happening to her? Where's she gone? Mother! Georgina! Where are you? Mr. Wonka, come quickly! Come here, Mr. Wonka! Something frightful's happened! Something's gone wrong. My old mother's disappeared!"

Mr. Wonka sighed and turned around and walked slowly and quite calmly back toward the bed.

"Where's my mother?" bawled Mrs. Bucket.

"Look at Josephine!" cried Grandpa Joe. "Just look at her! I ask you!"

Mr. Wonka looked first at Grandma Josephine. She was sitting in the middle of the huge bed, bawling her head off. "Wa! Wa! Wa!" she said. "Wa! Wa! Wa! Wa! Wa!"

"She's a screaming baby!" cried Grandpa Joe. "I've got a screaming baby for a wife!"

"The other one's Grandpa George!" Mr. Bucket said,

smiling happily. "The slightly bigger one there crawling around. He's my wife's father."

"That's right! He's my father!" wailed Mrs. Bucket. "And where's Georgina, my old mother? She's vanished! She's nowhere, Mr. Wonka! She's absolutely nowhere! I saw her getting smaller and smaller and in the end she got so small she just disappeared into thin air. What I want to know is where has she *gone?* And how in the world are we going to get her back?"

"Ladies and gentlemen," said Mr. Wonka, coming up close and raising both hands for silence. "*Please,* I beg you, do not ruffle yourselves! There's nothing to worry about."

"You call it nothing!" cried poor Mrs. Bucket. "When my old mother's gone up the spout and my father's a howling baby . . ."

"A lovely baby," said Mr. Wonka.

"I quite agree," said Mr. Bucket.

"What about my Josie?" cried Grandpa Joe.

"What *about* her?" said Mr. Wonka.

"Well . . ."

"A great improvement, sir," said Mr. Wonka, "don't you agree?"

"Oh, yes!" said Grandpa Joe. "I mean *NO!* What am I saying? She's a howling baby!"

"But in perfect health," said Mr. Wonka. "May I ask you, sir, how many pills she took?"

"Four," said Grandpa Joe glumly. "They all took four."

Mr. Wonka made a wheezing noise in his throat and a look of great anguish came over his face. "Why oh why can't people be more sensible?" he said sadly. "Why don't

they *listen* to me when I tell them something? I explained very carefully beforehand that each pill makes the taker exactly twenty years younger. So if Grandma Josephine took four of them, she automatically became younger by four times twenty, which is . . . wait a minute now . . . four twos are eight . . . add a nought . . . that's eighty . . . so she automatically became younger by eighty years. How old, sir, was your wife, if I may ask, before this happened?"

"She was eighty last birthday," Grandpa Joe answered. "She was eighty and three months."

"There you are, then!" cried Mr. Wonka, flashing a happy smile. "The Wonka-Vite worked perfectly. She is now precisely three months old! And a plumper, rosier infant I've never set eyes on!"

"Nor me," said Mr. Bucket. "She'd win a prize in any baby competition."

"*First* prize," said Mr. Wonka.

"Cheer up, Grandpa," said Charlie, taking the old man's hand in his. "Don't be sad. She's a beautiful baby."

"Madam," said Mr. Wonka, turning to Mrs. Bucket. "How old, may I ask, was Grandpa George, your father?"

"Eighty-one," wailed Mrs. Bucket. "He was eighty-one exactly."

"Which makes him a great big bouncing one-year-old boy now," said Mr. Wonka happily.

"How splendid!" said Mr. Bucket to his wife. "You'll be the first person in the world to change her father's diapers!"

"He can change his own rotten diapers!" said Mrs. Bucket. "What I want to know is *where's my mother?* *Where's* Grandma *Georgina?*"

"Ah-ha," said Mr. Wonka, "Oh-ho. . . . Yes, indeed, where oh where has Georgina gone? How old please, was the lady in question?"

"Seventy-eight," Mrs. Bucket told him.

"Well, of *course!*" laughed Mr. Wonka. "That explains it!"

"What explains what?" snapped Mrs. Bucket.

"My dear madam," said Mr. Wonka. "If she was only seventy-eight and she took enough Wonka-Vite to make her eighty years younger, then naturally she's vanished. She's bitten off more than she could chew! She's taken off more years than she had!"

"Explain yourself," said Mrs. Bucket.

"Simple arithmetic," said Mr. Wonka. "Subtract eighty from seventy-eight and what do you get?"

"Minus two!" said Charlie.

"Hooray!" said Mr. Bucket. "My mother-in-law's minus two years old!"

"Impossible!" said Mrs. Bucket.

"It's true," said Mr. Wonka.

"And where is she now, may I ask?" said Mrs. Bucket.

"That's a good question," said Mr. Wonka. "A very good question. Yes, indeed. Where is she now?"

"You don't have the foggiest idea, do you?"

"Of course I do," said Mr. Wonka. "I know exactly where she is."

"Then tell me!"

"You must try to understand," said Mr. Wonka, "that if she is now minus two, she's got to add two more years before she can start again from nought. She's got to wait it out."

"Where does she wait?" said Mrs. Bucket.

"In the Waiting Room, of course," said Mr. Wonka.

BOOM-BOOM! said the drums of the Oompa-Loompa band. BOOM-BOOM! BOOM-BOOM! And all the Oompa-Loompas, all the hundreds of them standing there in the Chocolate Room began to sway and hop and dance to the rhythm of the music. "Attention please!" they sang.

Attention please! Attention, please!
Don't dare to talk! Don't dare to sneeze!
Don't doze or daydream! Stay awake!
Your health, your very life's at stake!
Ho-ho, you say, they can't mean me.
Ha-ha, we answer, wait and see.
Did any of you ever meet
A child called Goldie Pinklesweet?
Who on her seventh birthday went
To stay with Granny down in Kent.
At lunchtime on the second day
Of dearest little Goldie's stay,
Granny announced, 'I'm going down
To do some shopping in the town.'
(D'you know why Granny didn't tell
The child to come along as well?
She's going to the nearest inn
To buy herself a double gin.)
So out she creeps. She shuts the door.
And Goldie, after making sure
That she is really by herself,
Goes quickly to the medicine shelf,
And there, her little greedy eyes
See pills of every shape and size,

Such fascinating colors, too—
Some green, some pink, some brown, some blue.
'All right,' she says, 'let's try the brown.'
She takes one pill and gulps it down.
'Yum-yum!' she cries. 'Hooray! What fun!
They're chocolate-coated, every one!'
She gobbles five, she gobbles ten,
She stops her gobbling only when
The last pill's gone. There are no more.
Slowly she rises from the floor.
She stops. She hiccups. Dear, oh dear,
She starts to feel a trifle queer.
You see, how could young Goldie know,
For nobody had told her so,
That Grandmama, her old relation
Suffered from frightful constipation.
This meant that every night she'd give
Herself a powerful laxative,
And all the medicines that she'd bought,
Were naturally of this sort.
The pink and red and blue and green
Were all extremely strong and mean,
But far more fierce and meaner still,
Was Granny's little chocolate pill.
Its blast effect was quite uncanny.
It used to shake up even Granny.
In point of fact she did not dare
To use them more than twice a year.
So can you wonder little Goldie
Began to feel a wee bit moldy?
Inside her tummy, something stirred.

A funny gurgling sound was heard,
And then, oh dear, from deep within,
The ghastly rumbling sounds begin!
They rumbilate and roar and boom!
They bounce and echo round the room!
The floorboards shake and from the wall
Some bits of paint and plaster fall.
Explosions, whistles, awful bangs
Were followed by the loudest clangs.
(A man next door was heard to say,
'A thunderstorm is on the way.')
But on and on the rumbling goes.
A window cracks, a lamp bulb blows.
Young Goldie clutched herself and cried,
'There's something wrong with my inside!'
This was, we very greatly fear,
The understatement of the year.
For wouldn't any child feel crummy,
With loud explosions in her tummy?
Granny, at half past two, came in,
Weaving a little from the gin,
But even so she quickly saw
The empty bottle on the floor.
'My precious laxatives!' she cried.
'I don't feel well,' the girl replied.
Angrily Grandma shook her head.
'I'm really not surprised,' she said.
'Why can't you leave my pills alone?'
With that, she grabbed the telephone
And shouted, 'Listen, send us quick

An ambulance! A child is sick!
It's number fifty, Fontwell Road!
Come fast! I think she might explode!'
We're sure you do not wish to hear
About the hospital and where
They did a lot of horrid things
With stomach pumps and rubber rings.
Let's answer what you want to know:
Did Goldie live or did she go?
The doctors gathered round her bed,
'There's really not much hope,' they said
'She's going, going, gone!' they cried.
She's had her chips! She's dead! She's died!'
'I'm not so sure,' the child replied,
And all at once she opened wide
Her great big bluish eyes and sighed,
And gave the anxious docs a wink,
And said, 'I'll be okay, I think.'
So Goldie lived and back she went
At first to Granny's place in Kent.
Her father came the second day
And fetched her in a Chevrolet,
And drove her to their home in Dover.
But Goldie's troubles were not over.
You see, if someone takes enough
Of any highly dangerous stuff,
One will invariably find
Some traces of it left behind.
It pains us greatly to relate
That Goldie suffered from this fate.

She'd taken such a massive fill
Of this unpleasant kind of pill,
It got into her blood and bones,
It messed up all her chromosomes,
It made her constantly upset,
And she could never really get
The beastly stuff to go away.
And so the girl was forced to stay
For seven hours every day
Within the everlasting gloom
Of what we call The Ladies Room.
And there she sits and dreams of glory,
Alone inside the lavatory.
So now, before it is too late.
Take heed of Goldie's dreadful fate.
And seriously, all jokes apart,
Do promise us across your heart
That you will never help yourself
To medicine from the medicine shelf.

16

Vita-Wonk and Minusland

"It's up to you, Charlie, my boy," said Mr. Wonka. "It's your factory. Shall we let your Grandma Georgina wait it out for the next two years, or shall we try to bring her back right now?"

"You don't really mean you might be able to bring her back?" cried Charlie.

"There's no harm in trying, is there . . . if that's the way you want it?"

"Oh yes, of course I do! For Mother's sake especially. Can't you see how sad she is?"

Mrs. Bucket was sitting on the edge of the big bed, dabbing her eyes with a hanky. "My poor old mother," she kept saying. "She's minus two and I won't see her again for months and months and months, if ever at all." Behind her, Grandpa Joe, with the help of an Oompa-Loompa, was feeding his three-month-old wife, Grandma Josephine, from a bottle. Alongside them, Mr. Bucket was spooning something called "Wonka's Squdgemallow Baby Food" into one-year-old Grandpa George's mouth but mostly all over his chin and chest. "Big deal," he was muttering angrily. "What a lousy rotten bust-up this is! They tell me I'm going to the chocolate factory to have a good time and I finish up being a mother to my father-in-law."

"Everything's under control, Charlie," said Mr. Wonka, surveying the scene. "They're doing fine. They don't need us here. Come along! We're off to hunt for Grandma!" He caught Charlie by the arm and went dancing toward the open door of the Great Glass Elevator. "Hurry up, my dear boy, hurry up!" he cried. "We've got to hustle if we're going to get there before!"

"Before *what*, Mr. Wonka?"

"Before she gets subtracted, of course! All Minuses are subtracted! Don't you know any arithmetic at all?"

They were in the Elevator now and Mr. Wonka was

searching among the hundreds of buttons for the one he wanted. "*Here* we are!" he said, placing his finger delicately upon a tiny ivory button on which it said "MINUSLAND."

The doors slid shut. And then, with a fearful whistling whirring sound the great machine leaped away to the right. Charlie grabbed Mr. Wonka's legs and held on tight. Mr. Wonka pulled a jump seat out of the wall and said, "Sit down, Charlie, quick, and strap yourself in tight! This journey's going to be rough and choppy!" There were straps on either side of the seat and Charlie buckled himself firmly in. Mr. Wonka pulled out a second seat for himself and did the same.

"We are going a long way down," he said "Oh, such a long way down we are going."

The Elevator was gathering speed. It twisted and swerved. It swung sharply to the left, then it went right, then left again, and it was heading downward all the time—down and down and down. "I only hope," said Mr. Wonka, "The Oompa-Loompas aren't using the other Elevator today."

"What other elevator?" asked Charlie.

"The one that goes the opposite way on the same track as this."

"Holy snakes, Mr. Wonka! You mean we might have a collision?"

"I've always been lucky so far, my boy. Hey! Take a look out there! Quick!"

Through the window, Charlie caught a glimpse of what seemed like an enormous quarry with a steep craggy-brown rock-face, and all over the rock-face there were hundreds of Oompa-Loompas working with picks and pneumatic drills.

"Rock candy," said Mr. Wonka. "That's the richest deposit of rock candy in the world."

The Elevator sped on. "We're going deeper, Charlie. Deeper and deeper. We're about two hundred thousand feet down already." Strange sights were flashing by outside but the Elevator was traveling at such terrific speed that only occasionally was Charlie able to recognize anything at all. Once, he thought he saw in the distance a cluster of tiny houses shaped like upside-down cups, and there were streets in between the houses and Oompa-Loompas walk-

ing in the streets. Another time, as they were passing some sort of a vast red plain dotted with things that looked like oil derricks, he saw a great spout of brown liquid spurting out of the ground high into the air. "A gusher!" cried Mr. Wonka, clapping his hands. "A whacking great gusher! How splendid! Just when we needed it!"

"A what?" said Charlie.

"We've struck chocolate again, my boy. That'll be a rich new field. Oh, what a beautiful gusher! Just look at it go!"

On they roared, heading downward more steeply than ever now, and hundreds, literally hundreds of astonishing sights kept flashing by outside. There were giant cogwheels turning and mixers mixing and bubbles bubbling and vast orchards of toffee-apple trees and lakes the size of football fields filled with blue and gold and green liquid, and everywhere there were Oompa-Loompas!

"You realize," said Mr. Wonka, "that what you saw earlier on when you went around the factory with all those naughty little children was only a tiny corner of the establishment. It goes down for miles and miles. And as soon as possible I shall show you all the way around slowly and properly. But that will take three weeks. Right now we have other things to think about and I have important things to tell you. Listen carefully to me, Charlie. I must talk fast, for we'll be there in a couple of minutes.

"I suppose you guessed," Mr. Wonka went on, "what happened to all those Oompa-Loompas in the Testing Room when I was experimenting with Wonka-Vite. Of course you did. They disappeared and became Minuses just like your Grandma Georgina. The recipe was miles too strong. One of them actually became minus eighty-seven! Imagine that!"

"You mean he's got to wait eighty-seven years before he can come back?" Charlie asked.

"That's what kept bugging me, my boy. After all, one can't allow one's best friends to wait around as miserable Minuses for eighty-seven years."

"And get subtracted as well," said Charlie. "That would be frightful."

"Of course it would, Charlie. So what did I do? 'Willy Wonka,' I said to myself, 'if you can invent Wonka-Vite to make people younger, then surely to goodness you can also invent something else to make people older!'"

"Ah-ha!" cried Charlie. "I see what you're getting at. Then you could turn the Minuses quickly back into Pluses and bring them home again."

"Precisely, my dear boy, precisely—always supposing, of course, that I could *find out* where the Minuses had gone to!"

The Elevator plunged on, diving steeply toward the center of the earth. All was blackness outside now. There was nothing to be seen.

"So once again," Mr. Wonka went on, "I rolled up my sleeves and set to work. Once again I squeezed my brain, searching for the new recipe. I had to create *age* . . . to make people *old, older, oldest.* . . . 'Ha-ha!' I cried, for now the ideas were beginning to come. 'What is the oldest living thing in the world? What lives longer than anything else?'"

"A tree," Charlie said.

"Right you are, Charlie! But what kind of a tree? Not the Douglas Fir. Not the Giant Redwood. Not the Sequoia. No, no, my boy. It is a tree called the Bristlecone Pine that grows upon the slopes of Wheeler Peak in Nevada, U.S.A. You can find Bristlecone Pines on Wheeler Peak today that are over four thousand years old! This is a fact, Charlie. Ask any dendrochronologist you like (and look that word up in the dictionary when you get home, will you please?). So that started me off. I jumped into the Great Glass Elevator and rushed all over the world collecting special items from the oldest living things . . .

A PINT OF SAP FROM A 4000-YEAR-OLD BRISTLECONE
    PINE.

THE TOENAIL CLIPPINGS FROM A 168-YEAR-OLD RUSSIAN
    FARMER CALLED PETROVITCH GREGOROVITCH.

AN EGG LAID BY A 200-YEAR-OLD TORTOISE BELONGING
    TO THE KING OF TONGA.

THE TAIL OF A 51-YEAR-OLD HORSE IN ARABIA.

THE WHISKERS OF A 36-YEAR-OLD CAT CALLED
    CRUMPETS.

AN OLD FLEA WHICH HAD LIVED ON CRUMPETS FOR
    36 YEARS.

THE TAIL OF A 207-YEAR-OLD GIANT RAT FROM TIBET.

THE BACK TEETH OF A 97-YEAR-OLD GRIMALKIN LIVING
    IN A CAVE ON MOUNT POPACATAPETAL.

THE KNUCKLEBONES OF A 700-YEAR-OLD CATTALOO
    FROM PERU . . .

All over the world, Charlie, I tracked down very old and ancient animals and took an important little bit of something from each one of them—a hair or an eyebrow, or sometimes it was no more than an ounce or two of toe-jam scraped from between its toes while it was sleeping. I tracked down THE WHISTLE-PIG, THE BOBOLINK, THE SKROCK, THE POLLYFROG, THE GIANT CURLICUE, THE STINGING SLUG AND

THE VENEOMOUS SQUERKLE WHO CAN SPIT POISON RIGHT INTO YOUR EYE FROM 50 YARDS AWAY. But there's no time to tell you about them all now, Charlie. Let me just say quickly that in the end, after lots of boiling and bubbling and mixing and testing in my Inventing Room, I produced one tiny cupful of oily black liquid and gave four drops of it to a brave twenty-year-old Oompa-Loompa volunteer to see what happened."

"What did happen?" Charlie asked.

"It was fantastic!" cried Mr. Wonka. "The moment he swallowed it, he began wrinkling and shriveling up all over and his hair started dropping off and his teeth started falling out and before I knew it, he had suddenly become an old fellow of seventy-five! And thus, my dear Charlie, was Vita-Wonk invented!"

"Did you rescue all the Oompa-Loompa Minuses, Mr. Wonka?"

"Every single one of them, my boy! One hundred and thirty-one all told! Mind you, it wasn't quite as easy as all that. There were lots of snags and complications along the way. Good heavens! We're nearly there. I *must* stop talking now and watch where we're going."

Charlie realized that the Elevator was no longer rushing and roaring. It was hardly moving at all now. It seemed to be drifting. "Undo your straps," Mr. Wonka said. "We must get ready for action." Charlie undid his straps and stood up and peered out. It was an eerie sight. They were drifting in a heavy gray mist and the mist was swirling and swishing around them as though driven by winds from many sides. In the distance, the mist was darker and almost black and it seemed to be swirling more fiercely than ever over there. Mr. Wonka slid open the doors. "Stand back!" he said. "Don't fall out, Charlie, whatever you do!"

The mist came into the Elevator. It had the fusty reeky smell of an old underground dungeon. The silence was overpowering. There was no sound at all, no whisper of wind, no voice of creature or insect, and it gave Charlie a queer frightening feeling to be standing there in the middle of this gray inhuman nothingness—as though he were in another world altogether, in some place where man should never be.

"Minusland," whispered Mr. Wonka. "This is it, Charlie. The problem now is to find her. We may be lucky. And then again, we may not."

17
Rescue in Minusland

"I DON'T LIKE IT here at all," Charlie whispered. "It gives me the willies."

"Me too," Mr. Wonka whispered back. "But we've got a job to do, Charlie, and we must go through with it."

The mist was condensing now on the glass walls of the Elevator, making it difficult to see out except through the open doors.

"Do any other creatures live here, Mr. Wonka?"

"Plenty of Gnoolies."

"Are they dangerous?"

"If they bite you, they are. You're a gonner, my boy, if you're bitten by a Gnooly."

The Elevator drifted on, rocking gently from side to side. The gray-black oily fog swirled around them.

"What does a Gnooly look like, Mr. Wonka?"

"They don't *look* like anything, Charlie. They can't."

"You mean you've never seen one?"

"You can't *see* Gnoolies, my boy. You can't even feel them . . . until they puncture your skin. Then it's too late. They've got you."

"You mean there might be swarms of them all around us this very moment?" Charlie asked.

"There might," said Mr. Wonka.

Charlie felt his skin beginning to creep. "Do you die at once?" he asked.

"First you become subtracted. . . . A little later you are divided . . . but very slowly. It takes a long time . . . it's long division and it's very painful. After that, you become one of them."

"Couldn't we shut the door?" Charlie asked.

"I'm afraid not, my boy. We'd never see her through the glass. There's too much mist and moisture. She's not going to be easy to pick out anyway."

Charlie stood at the open door of the Elevator and stared into the swirling vapors. This, he thought, is what hell must be like. Hell without heat. There was something unholy about it all, something unbelievably diabolical. It was all so deathly quiet, so desolate and empty. At the same time, the constant movement, the twisting and swirling of the misty vapors, gave one the feeling that some very powerful force, evil and malignant, was at work all around. Charlie felt a jab on his arm! He jumped! He almost jumped out of the Elevator! "Sorry," said Mr. Wonka. "It's only me."

"Oh-h-h!" Charlie gasped. "For a second, I thought . . ."

"I know what you thought, Charlie. . . . And by the way, I'm awfully glad you're with me. How would you like to come here alone as I did . . . as I had to many times?"

"I wouldn't," said Charlie.

"There she is," said Mr. Wonka, pointing. "No, she isn't! Oh, dear! I could have sworn I saw her for a moment right over there on the edge of that dark patch. Keep watching Charlie."

"There!" said Charlie. *"Over there!* Look!*"*

"Where?" said Mr. Wonka. "Point to her, Charlie!"

"She's . . . she's gone again. She sort of faded away," Charlie said.

They stood at the open door of the Elevator, peering into the swirly gray vapors.

"There! Quick! Right there!" Charlie cried. *"Can't you see her?"*

"Yes, Charlie! I see her! I'm moving up close now." Mr. Wonka reached behind him and began touching a number of buttons.

"Grandma!" Charlie cried out. "We've come to get you, Grandma!"

They could see her faintly through the mist, but oh so

faintly. And they could see the mist through *her* as well. She was transparent. She was hardly there at all. She was no more than a shadow. They could see her face and just the faintest outline of her body swathed in a nightgown. But she wasn't upright. She was floating lengthwise in the swirling vapor.

"Why is she lying down?" Charlie whispered.

"Because she's a Minus, Charlie. Surely you know what a minus sign looks like. . . . Like that." Mr. Wonka drew a horizontal line in the air with his finger.

The Elevator glided close. The ghostly shadow of Grandma Georgina's face was no more than a yard away now. Charlie reached out through the door to touch her but there was nothing there to touch. His hand went right through her skin. "Grandma!" he gasped. She began to drift away.

"Stand back!" ordered Mr. Wonka, and suddenly, from some secret place inside his coat-tails he whisked out a spraygun. It was one of those old-fashioned things people used to use for spraying fly spray around the room before Aerosol cans came along. He aimed the spraygun straight at the shadow of Grandma Georgina and he pumped the handle hard *once . . . twice . . . three times!* Each time, a fine black spray spurted out from the nozzle of the gun. Instantly, Grandma Georgina disappeared.

"A bulls-eye!" cried Mr. Wonka, jumping up and down with excitement. "I got her with both barrels. I plussed her good and proper. That's Vita-Wonk for you."

"Where's she gone?" Charlie asked.

"Back where she came from, of course. To the factory. She's a Minus no longer, my boy! She's a one hundred per-

cent red-blooded Plus! Come along now! Let's get out of here quickly before the Gnoolies find us!" Mr. Wonka jabbed a button. The doors closed and the Great Glass Elevator shot upward for home.

"Sit down and strap yourself in again, Charlie," said Mr. Wonka. "We're going flat out this time."

The Elevator roared and rocketed up toward the surface of the earth. Mr. Wonka and Charlie sat side by side on their little jump seats, strapped in tight. Mr. Wonka started tucking the spraygun back into that enormous pocket somewhere in his coat-tails. "It's such a pity one has to use a clumsy old thing like this," he said. "But there's simply no other way of doing it. Ideally, of course, one would measure out exactly the right number of drops into a teaspoon and feed it carefully into the mouth. But it's impossible to feed anything into a Minus. It's like trying to feed one's own shadow. That's why I've got to use a spraygun. Spray 'em all over, my boy! That's the only way!"

"It worked fine, though, didn't it?" Charlie said.

"Oh, it worked all right, Charlie! It worked beautifully! All I'm saying is there's bound to be a slight overdose . . ."

"I don't quite know what you mean, Mr. Wonka."

"My dear boy, if it only takes four drops of Vita-Wonk to turn a young Oompa-Loompa into an old man . . ." Mr. Wonka lifted his hands and let them fall limply onto his lap.

"You mean Grandma may have gotten too much?" asked Charlie, turning slightly pale.

"I'm afraid that's putting it rather mildly," said Mr. Wonka.

"But why did you give her such a lot of it then?" said Charlie, getting more and more worried. "Why did you spray her three times? She must have gotten pints and pints of it!"

"*Gallons!*" cried Mr. Wonka, slapping his thighs. "Gallons and gallons! But don't let a little thing like that bother you, my dear Charlie! The important part of it is we've got her back! She's a Minus no longer. She's a lovely Plus!

> *"She's as plussy as plussy can be!*
> *She's more plussy than you or than me!*
> *The question is how,*
> *Just how old is she now?*
> *Is she more than a hundred and three?"*

18

The Oldest Person
in the World

"WE RETURN IN TRIUMPH, Charlie!" cried Mr. Wonka as the Great Glass Elevator began to slow down. "Once more your dear family will all be together again!"

The Elevator stopped. The doors slid open. And there was the Chocolate Room and the chocolate river and the Oompa-Loompas and in the middle of it all the great bed belonging to the old grandparents. "Charlie!" said Grandpa Joe, rushing forward. "Thank heaven you're back!" Charlie hugged him. Then he hugged his mother and father. "Is she here?" he said. "Grandma Georgina?"

Nobody answered. Nobody did anything except Grandpa Joe, who pointed to the bed. He pointed but he didn't look where he was pointing. None of them looked at the bed—except Charlie. He walked past them all to get a better view, and he saw at one end the two babies, Grandma Josephine and Grandpa George, both tucked in and sleeping peacefully. At the other end . . .

"Don't be alarmed," said Mr. Wonka running up and placing a hand on Charlie's arm. "She's bound to be just a teeny bit over-plussed. I warned you about that."

"What have you done to her?" cried Mrs. Bucket. "My poor old mother!"

Propped up against the pillows at the other end of the bed was the most extraordinary thing Charlie had ever seen. Was it some ancient fossil? It couldn't be that because it was moving slightly. And now it was making sounds. Croaking sounds—the kind of sounds a very old frog might make if it knew a few words. "Well well well," it croaked. "If it isn't dear Charlie."

"Grandma!" cried Charlie. *"Grandma Georgina! Oh ... Oh ... Oh!"*

Her tiny face was like a pickled walnut. There were such masses of creases and wrinkles that the mouth and eyes and even the nose were sunken almost out of sight. Her hair was pure white and her hands, which were resting on top of the blanket, were just little lumps of wrinkly skin.

The presence of this ancient creature seemed to have terrified not only Mr. and Mrs. Bucket, but Grandpa Joe as well. They stood well back, away from the bed. Mr. Wonka, on the other hand, was as happy as ever. "My dear lady!" he cried advancing to the edge of the bed and clasping one of those tiny wrinkled hands in both of his. "Welcome home! And how are you feeling on this bright and glorious day?"

"Not too bad," croaked Grandma Georgina. "Not too bad at all, considering my age."

"Good for you!" said Mr. Wonka. "Atta girl! All we've got to do now is find out exactly how old you are! Then we shall be able to take further action!"

"You're taking no further action around here," said Mrs. Bucket, tight-lipped. "You've done enough damage already!"

"But my dear old muddleheaded mugwump," said Mr. Wonka, turning to Mrs. Bucket. "What does it matter that the old girl has become a trifle too old? We can put that right in a jiffy! Have you forgotten about Wonka-Vite and how every tablet makes you twenty years younger? We shall bring her back! We shall transform her into a blossoming blushing maiden in the twink of an eye!"

"What good is that when her husband's not even out of diapers yet?" wailed Mrs. Bucket, pointing a finger at the one-year-old Grandpa George, so peacefully sleeping.

"Madam," said Mr. Wonka, "let us do one thing at a time."

"I forbid you to give her that beastly Wonka-Vite!" said Mrs. Bucket. "You'll turn her into a Minus again just as sure as I'm standing here!"

"I don't want to be a Minus," croaked Grandma Georgina. "If I ever have to go back to that beastly Minusland again, the Gnoolies will griddle me."

"Fear not," said Mr. Wonka. "This time *I myself* will supervise the giving of the medicine. I shall personally see to it that you get the correct dosage. But listen very carefully now! I cannot work out how many pills to give you until I know exactly how old you are! That's obvious, isn't it?"

"It is not obvious at all," said Mrs. Bucket. "Why can't you give her one pill at a time and play it safe?"

"Impossible, madam. In very serious cases such as this, Wonka-Vite doesn't work at all when given in small doses. You've got to throw everything at her in one go. You've got to hit her with it hard. A single pill wouldn't even begin to shift her. She's too far gone for that. It's all or nothing."

"No," said Mrs. Bucket firmly.

"Yes," said Mr. Wonka. "Dear lady, please listen to me. If you have a very severe headache and you need *three* aspirins to cure it, it's no good taking only one at a time and waiting four hours between each. You'll never cure yourself that way. You've got to gulp them all down in one go. It's the same with Wonka-Vite. May I proceed?"

"Oh, all *right*, I suppose you'll have to," said Mrs. Bucket.

"Good," said Mr. Wonka, giving a little jump and twirling his feet in air. "Now then, how old are you, my dear Grandma Georgina?"

"I don't know," she croaked. "I lost count of that years and years ago."

"Don't you have *any* idea?" said Mr. Wonka.

"Of course I don't," gibbered the old woman. "Nor would you if you were as old as I am."

"Think!" said Mr. Wonka. "You've *got* to think!"

The tiny old wrinkled brown walnut face wrinkled itself up more than ever. The others stood waiting. The Oompa-Loompas, enthralled by the sight of this ancient object, were all edging closer and closer to the bed. The two babies slept on.

"Are you, for example, a hundred?" said Mr. Wonka. "Or a hundred and ten? Or a hundred and twenty?"

"It's no good," she croaked. "I never did have a head for numbers."

"This is a *catastrophe!*" cried Mr. Wonka. "If you can't tell me how old you are, I can't help you! I dare not risk an overdose!"

Gloom settled upon the entire company, including for once Mr. Wonka himself. "You've messed it up good and proper this time, haven't you?" said Mrs. Bucket.

"Grandma," Charlie said, moving forward to the bed. "Listen, Grandma. Don't worry about exactly how old you might be. Try to think of a *happening* instead. Think of something that *happened* to you. Anything you like . . . as far back as you can. It may help us."

"Lots of things happened to me, Charlie. So many many things happened to me . . ."

"But can you *remember* any of them, Grandma?"

"Oh, I don't know, my darling. I suppose I could remember one or two if I thought hard enough."

"Good, Grandma, good!" said Charlie eagerly. "Now what is the very earliest thing you can remember in your whole life?"

"Oh, my dear boy, that really would be going back a few years, wouldn't it?"

"When you were little, Grandma, like me. Can't you remember anything you did when you were little?"

The tiny sunken black eyes glimmered faintly and a sort of smile touched the corners of the almost invisible little slit of a mouth. "There was a ship," she said. "I can remember a ship. I couldn't ever forget that ship . . ."

"Go on, Grandma! A ship? What sort of a ship? Did you sail in her?"

"Of course I sailed in her, my darling. We all sailed in her."

"Where from? Where to?" Charlie went on eagerly.

"Oh no, I couldn't tell you that. I was just a tiny little girl." She lay back on the pillow and closed her eyes. Charlie watched her, waiting for something more. Everybody waited. No one moved.

"It had a lovely name, that ship. There was something beautiful, so beautiful about that name. But of course I couldn't possibly remember it . . ."

Charlie, who had been sitting on the edge of the bed, suddenly jumped up. His face was shining with excitement. "If I said the name, Grandma, would you remember it then?"

"I might Charlie . . . yes, I think I might . . ."

"The Mayflower!" cried Charlie.

The old woman's head jerked up off the pillow. *"That's it!"* she croaked. "You've *got* it, Charlie! The *Mayflower.* . . . Such a lovely name . . ."

"Grandpa!" Charlie called out, dancing with excitement. "What year did the *Mayflower* sail?"

"The *Mayflower* sailed out of Plymouth Harbor on September 6, 1620," said Grandpa Joe.

"Plymouth," croaked the old woman. "That rings a bell, too. Yes, it might easily have been Plymouth."

"Sixteen hundred and twenty!" cried Charlie. "Oh, my heavens above! That means you're . . . you do it, Grandpa!"

"Well now," said Grandpa Joe. "Take sixteen hundred and twenty away from nineteen hundred and seventy-two . . . that leaves . . . don't rush me now, Charlie. That leaves three hundred and fifty-two."

"Jumping jackrabbits!" yelled Mr. Bucket. "She's three hundred and fifty-two years old!"

"She's more," said Charlie. "How old did you say you were, Grandma, when you sailed on the *Mayflower?* Were you about eight?"

"I think I was even younger than that, my darling. I was only a little bitty girl, probably no more than six."

"Then she's *three hundred and fifty-eight!*" gasped Charlie.

"That's Vita-Wonk for you," said Mr. Wonka proudly. "I told you it was powerful stuff."

"Three hundred and fifty-eight," said Mr. Bucket. "It's unbelievable!"

"Just imagine the things she must have seen in her lifetime," said Grandpa Joe.

"My poor old mother!" wailed Mrs. Bucket. "What on earth . . ."

"Patience, dear lady," said Mr. Wonka. "Now comes the interesting part. Bring on the Wonka-Vite!"

An Oompa-Loompa ran forward with a large bottle and gave it to Mr. Wonka. He put it on the bed. "How young does she want to be?" he asked.

"Seventy-eight," said Mrs. Bucket firmly. "Exactly where she was before all this nonsense started."

"Surely she'd like to be a bit younger than that?" said Mr. Wonka.

"Certainly not!" said Mrs. Bucket. "It's too risky!"

"Too risky, too risky!" croaked Grandma Georgina. "You'll only minus me again if you try to be clever!"

"Have it your own way," said Mr. Wonka. "Now then, I've got to do a few sums." Another Oompa-Loompa trotted forward, holding up a blackboard. Mr. Wonka took a piece of chalk from his pocket and wrote:

Present age of person ... 358
Age she wants to be
    (subtract this) ... 78
Number of years younger
    she must become = 280
If each pill of Wonka-Vite makes
you 20 years younger, we must divide
280 by 20 to find out   14
how many pills to give: 20)280

"Fourteen pills of Wonka-Vite exactly," said Mr. Wonka. The Oompa-Loompa took the blackboard away. Mr. Wonka picked up the bottle from the bed and opened it and counted out fourteen of the little brilliant yellow pills. "Water!" he said. Another Oompa-Loompa ran forward with a glass of water. Mr. Wonka tipped all fourteen pills into the glass. The water bubbled and frothed. "Drink it while it's fizzing," he said, holding the glass up to Grandma Georgina's lips. "All in one gulp!"

She drank it.

Mr. Wonka sprang back and took a large brass clock from his pocket. "Don't forget," he cried, "it's a year a second! She's got two hundred and eighty years to lose!

That'll take her four minutes and forty seconds! Watch the centuries fall away!"

The room was so silent they could hear the ticking of Mr. Wonka's clock. At first nothing much happened to the ancient person lying on the bed. She closed her eyes and lay back. Now and again, the puckered skin of her face gave a twitch and her little hands jerked up and down, but that was all.

"One minute gone!" called Mr. Wonka. "She's sixty years younger."

"She looks just the same to me," said Mr. Bucket.

"Of course she does," said Mr. Wonka. "What's a mere sixty years when you're over three hundred to start with!"

"Are you all right, Mother?" said Mrs. Bucket anxiously. "Talk to me, Mother!"

"Two minutes gone!" called Mr. Wonka. "She's one hundred and twenty years younger!"

And now definite changes were beginning to show in the old woman's face. The skin was quivering all over and some of the deepest wrinkles were becoming less and less deep, the mouth less sunken, the nose more prominent.

"Mother!" cried Mrs. Bucket. "Are you all right? Speak to me, Mother, please!"

Suddenly, with a suddenness that made everyone jump, the old woman sat bolt upright in bed and shouted, *"We've beaten them! Yorktown's surrendered! We've kicked them out, those dirty British!"*

"She's going crazy!" said Mr. Bucket.

"Not at all," said Mr. Wonka. "She's going through the eighteenth century."

"Three minutes gone," said Mr. Wonka.

Every second now she was growing slightly less and less shriveled, becoming more and more lively. It was a marvelous thing to watch.

"Gettysburg!" she cried. *"General Lee is on the run!"*

And a few seconds later she let out a great wail of anguish and said, "He's dead, he's dead, he's dead!"

"Who's dead?" said Mr. Bucket, craning forward.

"Lincoln!" she wailed. *"There goes the train ..."*

"She must have seen it!" said Charlie. "She must have been there!"

"She *is* there," said Mr. Wonka. "At least she was a few seconds ago."

"Will someone please explain to me," said Mrs. Bucket, "what on earth ..."

"Four minutes gone!" said Mr. Wonka. "Only forty seconds left! Only forty more years to lose!"

"Grandma!" cried Charlie, running forward. "You're looking almost exactly like you used to! Oh, I'm so glad!"

"Just as long as it all stops when it's meant to," said Mrs. Bucket.

"I'll bet it doesn't," said Mr. Bucket. "Something always goes wrong."

"Not when *I'm* in charge of it, sir," said Mr. Wonka. "Time's up. She is now seventy-eight years old! How do you feel, dear lady? Is everything all right?"

"I feel tolerable," she said. "Just tolerable. But that's no thanks to you, you meddling old mackerel!"

There she was again, the same cantankerous grumbling old Grandma Georgina that Charlie had known so well before it all started. Mrs. Bucket flung her arms around her and began weeping with joy. The old woman pushed her aside and said, "What, may I ask, are those two silly babies doing at the other end of the bed?"

"One of them's your husband," said Mr. Bucket.

"Rubbish!" she said. "Where *is* George?"

"I'm afraid it's true, Mother," said Mrs. Bucket. "That's him on the left. The other one's Josephine."

"You . . . you chiseling old cheeseburger!" she shouted, pointing a fierce finger at Mr. Wonka. "What in the name of . . ."

"Now now now now now!" said Mr. Wonka. "Let us not for mercy's sake have another row so late in the day. If everyone will keep their hair on and leave this to Charlie and me, we shall have them exactly where they used to be in the flick of a fly's wing!"

19

The Babies Grow Up

"BRING ON THE VITA-WONK!" said Mr. Wonka. "We'll soon fix these two babies."

An Oompa-Loompa ran forward with a small bottle and a couple of silver teaspoons.

"Wait just one minute!" snapped Grandma Georgina. "What sort of devilish dumpery are you up to now?"

"It's all right, Grandma," said Charlie. "I promise you it's all right. Vita-Wonk does the opposite to Wonka-Vite. It makes you older. It's what we gave *you* when you were a Minus. It saved you!"

"You gave me too much!" snapped the old woman.

"We had to, Grandma."

"And now you want to do the same to Grandpa George!"

"Of course we don't," said Charlie.

"I wound up three hundred and fifty-eight years old," she went on. "What's to stop you making another little mistake and giving him *fifty times more than you gave me?* Then I'd suddenly have a twenty-thousand-year-old caveman in bed beside me! *Imagine that,* and him with a big knobby club in one hand and dragging me around by my hair with the other. No, thank you!"

"Grandma," Charlie said patiently. "With you we had to use a spray because you were a Minus. You were a ghost. But here Mr. Wonka can . . ."

"Don't talk to me about that man!" she cried. "He's batty as a bullfrog!"

"No, Grandma, he is *not!* And here he can measure it out exactly right, drop by drop, and feed it into their mouths. That's true isn't it, Mr. Wonka?"

"Charlie," said Mr. Wonka. "I can see that the factory is going to be in good hands when I retire. You learn very fast. I am so pleased I chose you, my dear boy, so very pleased. Now then, what's the verdict? Do we leave them as babies or do we grow them up with Vita-Wonk?"

"You go ahead, Mr. Wonka," said Grandpa Joe. "I'd like

you to grow my Josie up so she was just the same as before—eighty years old."

"Thank you, sir," said Mr. Wonka. "I appreciate the confidence you place in me. But what about the other one, Grandpa George?"

"Oh, all *right,* then," said Grandma Georgina. "But if he ends up a caveman I don't want him in *this* bed anymore!"

"That's settled then," said Mr. Wonka. "Come along, Charlie! We'll do them both together. You hold one spoon and I'll hold the other. I shall measure out four drops and four drops only into each spoon and we'll wake them up and pop it into their mouths."

"Which one shall I do, Mr. Wonka?"

"You do Grandma Josephine, the tiny one. I'll do Grandpa George, the one-year-old. Here's your spoon."

Charlie took the spoon and held it out. Mr. Wonka opened the bottle and dripped four drops of oily black liquid into Charlie's spoon. Then he did the same to his own. He handed the bottle back to the Oompa-Loompa.

"Shouldn't someone hold the babies while you give it?" said Grandpa Joe. "I'll hold Grandma Josephine."

"Are you mad?" said Mr. Wonka. "Don't you realize that Vita-Wonk acts instantly? It's not one year a second like Wonka-Vite. Vita-Wonk is as quick as lightning! The moment the medicine is swallowed–ping!–and it all happens! The getting bigger and the growing older and everything else all happens in one second. So don't you see, my dear sir," he said to Grandpa Joe, "that one moment you'd be holding a tiny baby in your arms and just one second

later you'd find yourself staggering about with an eighty-year-old woman and you'd drop her like a ton of bricks on the floor!"

"I see what you mean," said Grandpa Joe.

"All set, Charlie?"

"All set, Mr. Wonka." Charlie moved around the bed to where the tiny sleeping baby lay. He placed one hand behind her head and lifted it. The baby awoke and started yelling. Mr. Wonka was on the other side of the bed doing the same to one-year-old George. "Both together now, Charlie!" said Mr. Wonka. "Ready, steady, *go!* Pop it in." Charlie pushed his spoon into the open mouth of the baby and tipped the drops down her throat.

"Make sure she swallows it!" cried Mr. Wonka. "It won't work until it gets into their tummies!"

It is difficult to explain what happened next, and whatever it was, it only lasted for one second. A second is about as long as it takes you to say aloud and quickly, "one-two-three-four-five." And that is how long it took, with Charlie watching closely, for the tiny baby to grow and swell and wrinkle into the eighty-year-old Grandma Josephine. It was a frightening thing to see. It was like an explosion. A small baby suddenly exploded into an old woman, and Charlie all at once found himself staring straight into the well-known and much-loved wrinkly old face of his Grandma Josephine. *"Hello,* my darling," she said. "Where have *you* come from?"

"Josie!" cried Grandpa Joe, rushing forward. "How marvelous! You're back!"

"I didn't know I'd been away," she said.

Grandpa George had also made a successful comeback. "You were better-looking as a baby," Grandma Georgina said to him. "But I'm glad you've grown up again, George . . . for one reason."

"What's that?" asked Grandpa George.

"You won't wet the bed anymore."

20
How to Get Someone Out of Bed

"I AM SURE," said Mr. Wonka, addressing Grandpa George, Grandma Georgina and Grandma Josephine, "I am quite sure the three of you, after all that, will now want to jump out of bed and lend a hand in running the Chocolate Factory."

"Who, us?" said Grandma Josephine.

"Yes, you," said Mr. Wonka.

"Are you crazy?" said Grandma Georgina. "I'm staying right here where I am in this nice comfortable bed, thank you very much!"

"Me, too!" said Grandpa George.

At that moment, there was a sudden commotion among the Oompa-Loompas at the far end of the Chocolate Room. There was a buzz of excited chatter and a lot of running about and waving of arms, and out of all this a single Oompa-Loompa emerged and came rushing toward Mr. Wonka, carrying a huge envelope in his hands. He came up close to Mr. Wonka. He started whispering. Mr. Wonka bent down low to listen.

"Outside the factory gates?" cried Mr. Wonka. *"Men! . . . What sort of men? . . . Yes, but do they look dangerous? . . . Are they acting dangerously? And a what? . . . A helicopter! . . . And these men came out of it? . . . They gave you this?"*

Mr. Wonka grabbed the huge envelope and quickly slit it open and pulled out the folded letter inside. There was absolute silence as he skimmed swiftly over what was written on the paper. Nobody moved. Charlie began to feel cold. He knew something dreadful was going to happen. There was a very definite smell of danger in the air. The men outside the gates, the helicopter, the nervousness of the Oompa-Loompas . . . He was watching Mr. Wonka's face, searching for a clue, for some change in expression that would tell him how bad the news was.

"Great whistling whangdoodles!" cried Mr. Wonka, leaping so high in the air that when he landed his legs gave way and he crashed onto his backside.

"Snorting snozzwangers!" he yelled, picking himself up and waving the letter about as though he were swatting mosquitoes. "Listen to this, all of you. Just you listen to this!" He began to read aloud:

THE WHITE HOUSE
WASHINGTON D.C.

TO MR. WILLY WONKA.

SIR

TODAY THE ENTIRE NATION, INDEED THE WHOLE WORLD IS REJOICING AT THE SAFE RETURN OF OUR COMMUTER CAPSULE FROM SPACE WITH 136 SOULS ON BOARD. HAD IT NOT BEEN FOR THE HELP THEY RECEIVED FROM AN UNKNOWN SPACESHIP, THESE 136 PEOPLE WOULD NEVER HAVE COME BACK. IT HAS BEEN REPORTED TO ME THAT THE COURAGE SHOWN BY THE EIGHT ASTRONAUTS ABOARD THIS UNKNOWN SPACESHIP WAS EXTRAORDINARY. OUR RADAR STATIONS, BY TRACKING THIS SPACESHIP ON ITS RETURN TO EARTH, HAVE DISCOVERED THAT IT SPLASHED DOWN IN A PLACE KNOWN AS WONKA'S CHOCOLATE FACTORY. THAT, SIR, IS WHY THIS LETTER IS BEING DELIVERED TO YOU.

I WISH NOW TO SHOW THE GRATITUDE OF THE NATION BY INVITING ALL EIGHT OF THOSE INCREDIBLY BRAVE ASTRONAUTS TO COME AND STAY IN THE WHITE HOUSE FOR A FEW DAYS AS MY HONORED GUESTS.

I AM ARRANGING A SPECIAL CELEBRATION PARTY IN THE BLUE ROOM THIS EVENING AT WHICH I MYSELF WILL PIN MEDALS FOR BRAVERY UPON ALL EIGHT OF THESE GALLANT FLIERS. THE MOST IMPORTANT PERSONS IN THE LAND WILL BE PRESENT AT THIS GATHERING TO SALUTE THE HEROES WHOSE DAZZLING DEEDS WILL BE WRITTEN FOREVER IN THE HISTORY OF OUR NATION. AMONG THOSE ATTENDING WILL BE THE VICE-PRESIDENT, MISS ELVIRA TIBBS, ALL THE MEMBERS OF MY CABINET, THE CHIEFS OF THE ARMY, THE NAVY AND THE AIR FORCE, ALL MEMBERS OF THE CONGRESS, A FAMOUS SWORD SWAL-LOWER FROM AFGHANISTAN WHO IS NOW TEACHING ME TO EAT MY WORDS (WHAT YOU DO IS YOU TAKE THE S OFF THE BEGINNING OF THE SWORD AND PUT IT ON THE END BEFORE YOU SWALLOW IT). AND WHO ELSE IS COM-ING? OH YES, MY CHIEF INTERPRETER, AND THE GOVER-NORS OF EVERY STATE IN THE UNION, AND OF COURSE MY CAT, MRS. TAUBSYPUSS.

A HELICOPTER AWAITS ALL EIGHT OF YOU OUTSIDE THE FACTORY GATES. I MYSELF AWAIT YOUR ARRIVAL AT THE WHITE HOUSE WITH THE VERY GREATEST PLEASURE AND IMPATIENCE.

I BEG TO REMAIN, SIR.

MOST SINCERELY YOURS

Lancelot R. Gilligrass.

LANCELOT R. GILLIGRASS
President of the United States

P.S. COULD YOU PLEASE BRING ME A FEW WONKA FUDGE-
MALLOW DELIGHTS. I LOVE THEM SO MUCH BUT EVERY-
BODY AROUND HERE KEEPS STEALING MINE OUT OF THE
DRAWER IN MY DESK. AND DON'T TELL NANNY.

Mr. Wonka stopped reading. And in the stillness that
followed Charlie could hear people breathing. He could
hear them breathing in and out much faster than usual.
And there were other things, too. There were so many
feelings and passions and there was so much sudden
happiness swirling around in the air it made his head
spin. Grandpa Joe was the first to say something. . . .
"*Yippeeeeeeeeee!*" he yelled out, and he flew across the
room and caught Charlie by the hands and the two of
them started dancing away along the bank of the choco-

late river. "We're going, Charlie!" sang Grandpa Joe. "We're going to the White House after all!" Mr. and Mrs. Bucket were also dancing and laughing and singing, and Mr. Wonka ran all over the room proudly showing the President's letter to the Oompa-Loompas. After a minute or so, Mr. Wonka clapped his hands for attention. "Come along, come along!" he called out. "We mustn't dilly! We mustn't dally! Come on, Charlie! And you, sir, Grandpa Joe! And Mr. and Mrs. Bucket! The helicopter is outside the gates! We can't keep it waiting!" He began hustling the four of them toward the door.

"Hey!" screamed Grandma Georgina from the bed. "What about us? We were invited too, don't you forget that!"

"It said *all eight of us* were invited!" cried Grandma Josephine.

"And that includes *me!*" said Grandpa George.

Mr. Wonka turned and looked at them. "Of course it includes you," he said. "But we can't possibly get that bed into a helicopter. It won't go through the door."

"You mean . . . you mean if we don't get out of bed we can't come?" said Grandma Georgina.

"That's exactly what I mean," said Mr. Wonka. "Keep going Charlie," he whispered, giving Charlie a little nudge. "Keep walking toward the door."

Suddenly, behind them, there was a great *swoosh* of blankets and sheets and a pinging of bedsprings as the three old people all exploded out of the bed together. They came sprinting after Mr. Wonka, shouting, "Wait for us! Wait for us!"

It was amazing how fast they were running across the floor of the great Chocolate Room. Mr. Wonka and Charlie and the others stood staring at them in wonder. They leaped across paths and over bushes like gazelles in springtime, with their bare legs flashing and their nightshirts flying out behind them.

Suddenly Grandma Josephine put the brakes on so

hard she skidded five yards before coming to a stop. "Wait!" she screamed. "We must be mad! We can't go to a famous party in the White House in our nightshirts! We can't stand there practically naked in front of all those people while the President pins medals all over us!"

"Oh-h-h-h!" wailed Grandma Georgina. "Oh, what *are* we going to do?"

"Don't you have any clothes with you at all?" asked Mr. Wonka.

"Of course we don't!" said Grandma Josephine. "We haven't been out of that bed for twenty years!"

"We can't go!" wailed Grandma Georgina. "We'll have to stay behind!"

"Couldn't we buy something from a store?" said Grandpa George.

"What with?" said Grandma Josephine. "We don't have any money!"

"Money!" cried Mr. Wonka. "Good gracious me, don't you go worrying about money! I've got plenty of *that!*"

"Listen," said Charlie. "Why couldn't we ask the helicopter to land on the roof of a big department store on the way over. Then you can all pop downstairs and buy exactly what you want!"

"Charlie!" cried Mr. Wonka, grasping him by the hand. "What *would* we do without you? You're brilliant! Come along everybody! We're off to stay in the White House!"

They all linked arms and went dancing out of the Chocolate Room and along the corridors and out through the front door into the open where the big helicopter was waiting near the factory gates. A group of extremely important-looking gentlemen came toward them and bowed.

"Well, Charlie," said Grandpa Joe. "It's certainly been a busy day."

"It's not over yet," Charlie said, laughing. "It hasn't even begun."

AN INTERVIEW WITH
Roald Dahl

This interview, conducted by family friend Todd McCormack, took place in 1988, when Roald Dahl was 71. As Dahl himself said, "I have worked all my life in a small hut up in our orchard. It is a quiet private place and no one has been permitted to pry in there." He not only let Todd McCormack inside the hut, but also gave him rare insight into how he worked, where his ideas came from, and how he shaped them into unforgettable stories. Roald Dahl passed away in 1990, two years after the interview.

WHAT IS IT LIKE WRITING A BOOK?

When you're writing, it's rather like going on a very long walk, across valleys and mountains and things, and you get the first view of what you see and you write it down. Then you walk a bit further, maybe up onto the top of a hill, and you see something else. Then you write that and you go on like that, day after day, getting different views of the same landscape really. The highest mountain on the walk is obviously the end of the book, because it's got to be the best view of all, when everything comes together and you can look back and see that everything you've done all ties up. But it's a very, very long, slow process.

HOW DO YOU GET THE IDEAS FOR YOUR STORIES?

It starts always with a tiny little seed of an idea, a little germ, and that even doesn't come very easily. You can be mooching around for a year or so before you get a good one. When I do get a good one, mind you, I quickly write it down so that I won't forget it, because it disappears otherwise rather like a dream. But when I get it, I don't dash up here and start to write it. I'm very careful. I walk around it and look at it and sniff it and then see if I think it will go. Because once you start, you're embarked on a year's work and so it's a big decision.

HOW DID YOU GET THE IDEA FOR
JAMES AND THE GIANT PEACH?

I had a kind of fascination with the thought that an apple—there're a lot of apple trees around here, and fruit trees, and you can watch them through the summer getting bigger and bigger from a tiny little apple to bigger and bigger ones, and it seemed to me an obvious thought—what would happen if it didn't stop growing? Why should it stop growing at a certain size? And this appealed to me and I thought this was quite a nice little idea and [then I had to think] of which fruit I should take for my story. I thought apple, pear, plum, peach. Peach is rather nice, a lovely fruit. It's pretty and it's big and it's squishy and you can go into it and it's got a big seed in the middle that you can play with. And so the story started.

WHAT IS YOUR WORK ROUTINE?

My work routine is very simple and it's always been so for the last 45 years. The great thing, of course, is never to work too long at a stretch, because after about two hours you are not at your highest peak of concentration, so you have to stop. Some writers choose certain times to write, others [choose] other times, and it suits me to start rather late. I start at 10 o'clock and I stop at 12. Always. However well I'm going, I will stay there until 12, even if I'm a bit stuck. You have to keep your bottom on the chair and stick it out. Otherwise, if you start getting in the habit of walking away, you'll never get it done.

HOW DO YOU KEEP THE MOMENTUM GOING WHEN YOU ARE WRITING A NOVEL?

One of the vital things for a writer who's writing a book, which is a lengthy project and is going to take about a year, is how to keep the momentum going. It is the same with a young person writing an essay. They have got to write four or five or six pages. But when you are writing it for a year, you go away and you have to come back. I never come back to a blank page; I always finish about halfway through. To be confronted with a blank page is not very nice. But Hemingway, a great American writer, taught me the finest trick when you are doing a long book, which is, he simply said in his own words, "When you are going good, stop writing." And that means that if everything's going well and you know exactly where the end of the chapter's going to go and you know just what the people are going to do, you don't go on writing and writing until you come to the end of it, because when you do, then you say, well, where am I going to go next? And you get up and you walk away and you don't want to come back because you don't know where you want to go. But if you stop when you are going good, as Hemingway said…then you know what you are going to say next. You make yourself stop, put your pencil down and everything, and you walk away. And you can't wait to get back because you know what you want to say next and that's lovely and you have to try and do that. Every time, every day all the way through the year. If you stop when you are stuck, then you are in trouble!

WHAT IS THE SECRET TO KEEPING YOUR READERS ENTERTAINED?

My lucky thing is I laugh at exactly the same jokes that children laugh at and that's one reason I'm able to do it. I don't sit out here roaring with laughter, but you have wonderful inside jokes all the time and it's got to be exciting, it's got to be fast, it's got to have a good plot, but it's got to be funny. It's got to be funny. And each book I do is a different level of that. Oh, *The Witches* is quite different from *The BFG* or *James [and the Giant Peach]* or *Danny [the Champion of the World]*. The line between roaring with laughter and crying because it's a disaster is a very, very fine one. You see a chap slip on a banana skin in the street and you roar with laughter when he falls slap on his backside. If in doing so you suddenly see he's broken a leg, you very quickly stop laughing and it's not a joke anymore. I don't know, there's a fine line and you just have to try to find it.

HOW DO YOU CREATE INTERESTING CHARACTERS?

When you're writing a book, with people in it as opposed to animals, it is no good having people who are ordinary, because they are not going to interest your readers at all. Every writer in the world has to use the characters that have something interesting about them, and this is even more true in children's books. I find that the only way to make my characters *really* interesting to children is to exaggerate all their good or bad qualities, and so if a person is nasty or bad or cruel, you make them very nasty, very bad, very cruel. If they are ugly, you make them extremely ugly. That, I think, is fun and makes an impact.

HOW DO YOU INCLUDE HORRIFIC EVENTS WITHOUT SCARING YOUR READERS?

You never describe any horrors happening, you just say that they do happen. Children who got crunched up in Willy Wonka's chocolate machine were carried away and that was the end of it. When the parents screamed, "Where has he gone?" and Wonka said, "Well, he's gone to be made into fudge," that's where you laugh, because you don't see it happening, you don't hear the child screaming or anything like that ever, ever, ever.

How much has living in the countryside influenced you?

I wouldn't live anywhere else except in the country, here. And, of course, if you live in the country, your work is bound to be influenced by it in a lot of ways, not pure fantasy like Charlie with chocolate factories, witches, and BFG's, but the others that are influenced by everything around you. I suppose the one [book] that is most dependent purely on this countryside around here is *Danny the Champion of the World,* and I rather love that book. And when I was planning it, wondering where I was going to let Danny and his father live, all I had to do, I didn't realize it, all I had to do was look around my own garden and there it was.

Roald Dahl on the subject of chocolate:

In . . . seven years of this glorious and golden decade [the 1930s], all the great classic chocolates were invented: the Crunchie, the Whole Nut bar, the Mars bar, the Black Magic assortment, Tiffin, Caramello, Aero, Malteser, the Quality Street assortment, Kit Kat, Rolo, and Smarties. In music the equivalent would be the golden age when compositions by Bach and Mozart and Beethoven were given to us. In painting it was the equivalent of the Renaissance in Italian art and the advent of the Impressionists toward the end of the nineteenth century. In literature it was Tolstoy and Balzac and Dickens. I tell you, there has been nothing like it in the history of chocolate and there never will be.

Roald Dahl, born in 1916 in
Wales, spent his childhood in England and later
worked in Africa. When World War II broke
out, he joined the Royal Air Force and became
a fighter pilot. After a war injury, he moved
to Washington, D.C., and there he began to
write. His first short story was published by
The Saturday Evening Post, and so began a long
and distinguished career.

Roald Dahl became, quite simply, one of
the best-loved children's book authors of all
time. Although he passed away in 1990, his
popularity and that of his many books—*Charlie
and the Great Glass Elevator, James and the Giant Peach,
Danny the Champion of the World,* to name just a
few—continues to grow.

Visit www.roalddahl.com to learn more about
the author and his books.

Quentin Blake has
illustrated most of Roald Dahl's children's
books as well as many others. The Children's
Laureate of the United Kingdom and a
recipient of the Kate Greenaway Medal,
Quentin Blake lives in London and teaches
illustration at the Royal College of Art.